MW01051540

Sudden Summer

Gilda Harrington

bANNed books
AustiN, Texas

FIRST EDITION

A Banned Book

Copyright © 1991
by Gilda Harrington

Published in the United States of America
By Edward-William Publishing Company
Number 292, P.O. Box 33280, Austin, Texas 78764

All Rights Reserved. No part of this book may be reproduced in any form without written permission from the publisher, except for brief passages included in a review appearing in a newspaper or magazine.

ISBN 0-934411-39-5

For SLK, who helped with the research

CHAPTER ZERO

Suddenly it was summer, a hot and humid Southern summer. The kind of summer I always think you survive rather than savor. So when Dawn called me at home that morning and suggested we eat our bag lunches together at the Pigeon Park, of course I accepted immediately.

I like Dawn. She's large and strong and funny. She wears clothes the way most people hang them to dry, but after two minutes in her company, how she looks has nothing to do with anything at all. A wonderful, warm woman like Dawn is someone you look to for a friend, not a pin-up.

"Hi, Rosie," she called to me as I ran towards her bench. Pigeon Park is within walking distance of our factories, but I have a tendency to be late for things. Luckily, my friends have a tendency to forgive me.

"Peanut butter and tuna fish again?" I asked, taking out my own sandwich and sitting down.

Dawn nodded. "Gotta feed my phobias."

This was her standard joke but, still, I laughed. "Like what? Fear of flying?" I teased.

"More like fear of diving, right now, though the only body of water within spitting distance of Bigstone is mine," she roared. "I'm sweating like hell in this humidity."

"So am I. Two weeks of record high temperatures, and the weatherman says no relief in sight. The biggest drought since the depression, they're saying."

"Pretty soon," said Dawn, biting into a juicy tomato, "they'll have to send in the Marines."

"Very funny," I said, trying to keep a straight face.

"So what's new, Rosie? Heard anything about the promotion?"

"No, just about the layoffs."

"Say what?"

"The boss just announced that they're moving soon, to North Carolina."

"How soon?"

"A few months."

"What's North Carolina got that we haven't?" Dawn asked.

"It's the other way around."

"What do you mean?"

"I mean that North Carolina is non-union. That's why lots of movie companies are going there to shoot, and that's why textile and food factories, you know, labor-intensive kinds of businesses, are moving there by the trainload these days."

"How do you know all this?" Dawn queried. I wasn't famous for my academic skills, that's for sure, and she was surprised.

"I do my homework," I replied.

It was Dawn's turn to laugh, and I didn't blame her. I was never all that great a student. In fact I barely graduated high school, and homework was right up there with the bubonic plague in my book.

But ever since I joined the union and started to go to meetings, I took a great interest in labor relations and did a lot of reading and listening. I had a lot to learn but, for the first time in my life, I found something that grabbed my interest and actually made me eager to learn.

Dawn knew this, too. "You're changing, Rosie. You're growing up."

I must have blushed because she went on quickly, touching my hand. "I like it. Hell, I like you, just the way

2

you are or any way you'll become. This union stuff's doing you a lot of good, I can see that."

"It's interesting," I said lamely. "It's meaningful. I can see myself becoming a real organizer, you know? Going around from place to place, talking to people, making them see they're getting the short end of every stick, every time — if they're just looking out for Number One instead of for everyone . . .''

I saw by the look on Dawn's face that I'd lost one potential convert already. "Sorry. I get real preachy sometimes."

"You're the strangest woman I ever met, Rosie, and that's a fact," Dawn said, wiping some juice from her chin and chest. "I swear I don't know where you'll end up, but I bet it won't be boring there, that's for sure."

"Amen. Whisper that in God's ear, girl, and may my wish come true." I put the apple back in my bag; it didn't tempt me in the least. "I hate it here."

"Nothing to hate, nothing to love."

"That's what I mean."

Dawn roared with laughter. "I can just see you in some awful maudlin melodrama, playing the stupid, starry-eyed leading lady and fainting away at the end of every scene."

I was more than happy to oblige that fantasy and, putting on my sweetest voice, I said: "Oh, Edward, my love, my man, was that really your mouth on mine?'"

"Swoon, swoon," Dawn commented with a smile, playing along. Then, giving vent to her true emotions, she added in a serious voice: "How disgusting."

"Well, at least these days, sometimes, playwrights come up with better lines for women," I ventured.

I never could figure out if Dawn had any political feelings at all, or what they were, so I ended up never broaching that subject with her at all. It didn't dampen our friendship one bit, because politics was one subject I kept pretty much to myself in Bigstone. And I was right, wasn't I? Dawn was my best friend, and even she got bored when I talked union.

"These new lines may sound different, but they're basically still the same lines," Dawn argued. "Baby lines."

I was really confused. What was this all about? "Baby lines? What do you mean?"

"Whatever the plot, whatever the words — in the end, movie women all end up in line for a baby," she said in a voice that felt both sad and wise.

"So what's wrong with that? I thought that's what all women did want," I said, looking at my watch, the one Carl gave me for my birthday the month before we broke up.

"Don't you?" I added.

"The question isn't really whether all women want babies, but why and how," she replied, gathering herself up.

Then she seemed to soften a bit and to think something over before speaking to me again. "You like music?"

"I love music. You know I love music, Dawn. What's up?"

"Actually, I just had an idea."

"Fancy," I teased.

"I'm serious. Don't faint. Some people I know are driving down from North Carolina and picking me up on their way to a music festival. A women's festival," she added, shifting her balance from foot to foot. "You know, just for women."

"And?" I prompted. I didn't understand the hemming and the hawing.

"And these friends," Dawn went on, her eyes riveted to her sneakers, "they have this extra ticket, so it suddenly hit me that maybe you'd like to come with us."

"When?"

"This weekend. You'd have to take Friday off, 'cause we're leaving Thursday evening." She squinted at me. "A hundred bucks, that's the price for the entire weekend, but if you can't afford it they'll take less, see, 'cause it's already paid for and otherwise it's a total loss anyway."

I didn't wait to think it over. I agreed at once. Call it luck, call it destiny — whatever. The rest is . . . well, my story.

CHAPTER ONE

It wasn't hard for me to get some time off from work. In fact, under the circumstances the difficult part was to make sure I had a job to come back to on Tuesday.

But what the hell, I was happy for the chance to get out of Bigstone and get into some good music. I could hardly wait to meet Dawn after work the next day to talk about it some more.

When Dawn and I met for beers that evening to make final plans, the bar was already smokey, and several men were already on their way to the floor. We found a relatively quiet corner and sat down.

"Funny how long we've known each other, Rosie," Dawn began, after the first full sip. "And how little we really know about each other."

"Not much to know," I said vaguely.

"You know what I mean. To you I'm just a big, blustering woman, right?" Dawn said, drinking her beer a little too fast and signalling Helen, the waitress, for another. "And who are you? A small town girl with big city dreams? Or some other cliche?"

"Come on, you've known me all your life. Almost," I amended. Both of us were born and raised in Bigstone, a small town on the edge of nowhere. Dawn's father left her mother almost as soon as she came home from the hospital with their baby, and moved to Texas. Many years later, someone passing through town brought us the news that Tom Wilson had become a successful rancher down

there. Not that long afterwards, he sent Dawn a short note—
and some money—asking her to come and visit.

Dawn went to Texas that summer during school vacation. She was sixteen and somewhat of a misfit: sort of
big physically and definitely small emotionally. A bit of
a baby, in fact.

Next thing anybody knew, Dawn Wilson was twenty
years old and back in town. Nobody quite knew why. She
didn't volunteer any information about her four-year ab-
sence, or the reasons for her return, and nobody felt it
was right to ask.

Meanwhile, her mother had remarried and moved to
his house in the next county, leaving the old family house
to the weeds and the sand.

Nobody had moved into Bigstone for years, and certainly nobody had ever moved back until Dawn showed
up that day in her overalls and boots, her hair trailing
wildly to all sides of the vintage motorcycle she was driving. The black sidecar was full of everything she owned
in the world.

Not much.

Dawn had a tremendous amount of energy and
strength. Within a month, the dilapidated Wilson shack
was transformed into a beautiful little house and she was
starting a vegetable garden in the back yard.

It didn't take the local gossips long to start making
up stories about Dawn Wilson. These were strange and
silly tales that had her either eloping with an oil man only
to be dumped "just like her poor Mama," or being rejected
by one cad after another until she grew to hate all men,
eventually returning to Bigstone for solitary solace. Some
whispered that she had had a baby out of wedlock, and
some even dared to whisper the word "abortion." Her
mother never came to visit and, as far as I could tell, Dawn
never went to see her, either. The word from the postman
was that she never wrote to, or got a letter from, her father
in Texas.

Some people stayed clear of her, feeling uncomfortable for some reason, I guess, but I had always liked Dawn when we were in school, and we became friends all over again when she came back.

Dawn broke into my daydream. "That's true enough," she said in her big voice. "We've known each other a long time. But I'm not sure I really know much about you. I mean about what you really feel, not just what you say and what you do."

"Bigstone isn't exactly the kind of place for mysteries, secrets, and dark corners," I said in exasperation. What the hell was going on, anyway?

She was gulping down the second bottle as easily as if it were soda pop. I wasn't too happy with the situation. I'm not a drinker. I can get through a beer or a glass of wine in an evening, but that's pushing it, and people who drink more than I do always make me nervous. "But then again," she continued, "you don't know anything about me, either."

"I never pry," I said quickly, but I guess my eyes told the story my lips never dared: I was curious.

Dawn was in the mood to oblige. "I'm lesbian," she whispered hoarsely.

I grabbed the waitress as she passed us again, paid, and practically pushed Dawn out of the place ahead of me. Once outside, we looked at each other for a minute, breathing hard.

"I thought you were my friend, Rosie."

"I am. Let's go."

I pushed her into my car and drove to the park. It was early evening, and nobody was around.

"I'm lesbian, my friends are lesbians, and at the festival there will be thousands of lesbians. I just wanted you to know, Rosie. That's all."

"You're wild, Dawn, but I never figured you for a queer."

"I'm not. I'm normal. What's so abnormal about loving women? Nobody thinks twice about it when men do it," she said, and burped.

"You drink too much."

"That should be my biggest problem."

"It scares me."

"That I'm lesbian?"

"That you drink."

"Ha!" But she let it go. "It's under control, anyway," she added.

We sat in silence in the darkness for a few minutes.

"I don't know if I should go to this music festival after all," I ventured at last.

"You need a vacation."

"I'm not sure it'll be a vacation."

"What do you think, that a bunch of fuzzy females will try to seduce you?"

I blushed, probably. I never talk about sex. "Not really."

"What, then? That nobody will try to seduce you?"

"You're disgusting, Dawn."

"Listen, I'm sorry. I am, Rosie. I like you a lot, you're the only person here who's real to me, and I guess I needed to tell somebody. I made a mistake. I'm sorry."

I took a deep breath. "I like you too. You know I do. But I never . . ."

"Don't worry about it. I never felt like making love with you, either. We're practically sisters. It would be like incest, wouldn't it?"

And then she began to cry, and I held her head to my chest. There must have been a bit of moon, because I remember her hair shining at me as I stroked it. She cried for a long, long time.

"I never told anyone," she whispered then. "Not anyone."

"It's okay, Dawn. Really. It's okay. I don't care if you're a lesbian, I'm still your friend."

She cried again, and I held her closer. Out of the corner of my eye I noticed the first carful of teenagers driving

9

towards Lovers' Lane, and I must have stiffened, because Dawn got up very quickly. Our heads collided.

"Company," I said.

She wiped her eyes with the back of her shirtsleeve. "Let's go home."

I drove her back to the bar. She got onto her motorcycle.

"Here," she added, stuffing a piece of paper into my pocketbook. "Here's a list of what you'll need to bring along."

"Please come," she said softly.

I nodded slowly. She seemed to brighten up a bit.

"Come over to my house as soon as you get off work tomorrow. I promise, Rosie, you'll I have the best vacation of your life."

She roared off, and I drove slowly to my parents' house.

CHAPTER TWO

Dawn's friends didn't look any queerer than I did. What made these women lesbians, anyway?

"Got everything?" Dawn asked as soon as she introduced me to Cathy and to Meg.

"Yes."

"Then let's boogie," she said, stuffing our backpacks into her friends' station wagon.

On the way south, they put on some music for me to hear, to give me a "quick lesson in women's culture," as Meg put it. She was a very good driver, but the fact that she kept caressing Cathy with one hand all the time made me uneasy.

The music was fine, but the lyrics were strange. Dawn made it worse by pointing out the obvious, that these were love songs sung by women for women, but at least she kept her hands to herself.

Finally, we arrived at the festival site. It was late, it was night, and we were given directions to our half of the cabin and to the parking area.

The cabin was all right. I'd seen worse. Each of us had half of a bunk bed and we had to share the bathroom with the four women who slept in the other half of the cabin. They were out.

Dawn said that they were probably at the dance and asked, "Why don't we go?"

So we took showers, changed, and walked over to the dance. The three of them had been to this festival before,

11

it was an annual event apparently, and knew the place like the palms of their hands. This was a point of pride.

When we got to the main stage, a live band was playing. As you've already guessed, the band was made up only of women. And so were those who worked the lights and the sound. It was quite strange.

But for me, the strangest thing of all was seeing hundreds and hundreds of women dancing together.

Don't get me wrong, I'd seen women dancing together before. In our town, it's quite common for women to dance together if there aren't enough men to go around. But this was different.

They were dancing the way people in movies make love, they were all over each other. I admit it made me nervous. I had that funny feeling again all over, like the night before, and I still had no idea what it was.

"Wanna dance?"

She was tall and beautiful. Her blonde hair was long and hung softly about her bare shoulders like freshly harvested hay. Her high cheekbones set off her blue eyes like a framed work of art, and her —

"Wanna dance?" she repeated with a smile.

Before I knew what was going on, she had me on the dance floor with my arms around her body.

"I'm Calypso. What's your name?"

"Rose. Rosie Malone."

"Irish?"

"Somewhat."

"First time?"

I nodded.

"Lucky," she said, and spun me around.

"Why lucky?" I managed to ask at last. Call me curious.

"Because this is the most exciting thing around, a festival just for us girls, for making beautiful music together. I envy you, because for you it's all new and wonderful."

I had to laugh. "Believe me, having someone envy me is new and wonderful."

She laughed along. "What are friends for?"

And the song was over, and she was gone.

I almost missed her, but then Dawn materialized and grabbed me for the next dance.

"Who was that?" she asked.

"What are you talking about?"

"Ugh," she went on, almost spitting from disgust. "I hate dykes that can make the cover of *Vogue* magazine. It's obscene."

My thoughts drifted until I felt her stepping on my foot.

"Ouch!"

She took a step back but kept the rhythm. "So how do you like it here? A big step from Bigstone, that's for sure."

We laughed.

"You have possibilities, Rosie. We'll make a dyke out of you yet."

Then she noticed that I was paling, and said quickly: "Don't take it so hard. I meant it as a compliment."

Cathy and Meg came over, holding hands.

"So how's the water, Rosie?" asked Meg.

"That was a quick fancy dive, there," Cathy advised. "Watch out!"

And with a giggle, they were gone.

"Don't mind them," Dawn said. "They've been together forever and have a maternal interest in every female they meet."

We went over to the concession area for a drink. Some of the women had no tops on, and I alternated between staring and shyness.

"Why do you use the word 'dyke,' Dawn?" I had to ask. "It's like a black person saying 'colored', or 'Negro', isn't it?"

"It's not the word, honey, it's the inflection. You can call me lesbian, Amazon, hag, crone, witch, Earth Mother, goddess, or dyke for that matter, and if your heart is friendly, it'll be fine with me."

13

The line in front of us at the concession stand had dwindled by then, and we got our sodas.

"Let's take a walk," Dawn suggested, and we did. The air smelled fresh and wonderful. I could feel the water, and wanted to get nearer.

"There's a lake out there," Dawn cautioned. "You know how I feel about water."

"C'mon, chicken, I won't push you in. I promise." I took her arm and gave her a playful shove. "I love lakes. Do it for me, okay?"

Dawn finally agreed to go. When we got to the lake, I saw that there were all kinds of tents in many shapes, colors, and sizes nearby. Somewhere, someone was singing and playing a guitar. It was peaceful.

We walked along the lakefront until we came to a wooden dock and followed it to the end, where we sat down.

"I love it here," Dawn said softly, almost to the wind. "No matter what my real feelings, and they're usually pretty bad, I always feel happy here."

"You don't mean the lake, I gather."

She smiled. "No. I mean the land. The festival."

"It's a pretty place."

"It's more than just a pretty place. It's home. A generic home, Everywoman's home, somewhere where every woman can just be herself and do whatever the hell she wants."

"You *always* do what you want," I pointed out.

"That's what you think."

"That's what I know. Ever since you came back, you've lived your own life and gone pretty much your own way. In Bigstone, Dawn, that spells independence."

"It spells shit," she replied, and this time she did spit, right into the beautiful calm water. "It spells nothing. I live in the closet."

"You live in a house of your own. I wish I had that!"

"I live in the biggest, most comfortable closet around, but it's still a closet and it's still stifling."

14

"What closet, Dawn? What are you talking about?"

"A closet is where you hang things. For us dykes, a closet is where we hang ourselves every day when we leave the house. We hang our real self in the closet and put on our mask, our masquerade self, in order to face the so-called real world."

"That's a great speech, Dawn, but it's phony," I confronted her. "What mask? What masquerade? Why, you're the most outspoken, free-wheeling, devil-may-care woman in the county!"

"Maybe," she allowed. "Maybe. But I'm in hiding all the time. Nobody knows the real me, the woman-loving-woman me."

"Big deal."

"It is. For me. And it's a big deal to you, too. I bet you're scared I'd kiss you, or something."

"Not scared, exactly."

"Repulsed?"

"No. I guess I'm just confused." I stared at the shimmering water and wished I had a stone to skip. "I've never thought about all this before. I never met a lesbian before in my life."

"Ha! You've met plenty."

"Who?"

"That's not the point, Rosie. We're not talking gossip, we're talking life. Ten women in a hundred are dykes, so figure out how many of us there are in Bigstone, population 1327. And if your math isn't too good, and as I remember it isn't, then it comes out to about seventy women."

"You're kidding!"

"I'm not. Who knows? We are everywhere!" and she laughed.

I was genuinely puzzled. For a minute, the face of Miss Sawyer, the gym teacher, flashed before me. I blushed to realize that she was at the top of my list of likely Bigstone candidates for lesbians. I wondered who her lover was, if this was true, and blushed even harder when I looked at Dawn again.

"What you thinking, girl?"

"Nothing," I replied hastily.

Just then, Cathy and Meg joined us on the dock.

"Thought we'd find you here!" Meg exclaimed in triumph.

"How's the baby dyke?" Cathy asked cryptically.

"So far, so good," Dawn answered, equally in code.

"What's all this baby talk?" I blurted.

They laughed.

"We're talking about you," Meg said. "An up-and-coming lesbian, that's who we call a baby dyke."

I was annoyed. "Is that how you get your statistics? All women who are not involved with men at any given time are lesbians?" I asked. "Well, I'm not a lesbian, and I'm not a baby!"

"Right," Cathy replied calmly, taking off her blouse. Meg massaged her back while she went on: "It's just a feeling. I may be wrong. Nine times out of ten, my intuition's awesome, but now and again I let my imagination run wild."

"Don't worry about it if it bothers you," Meg offered.

I was left hurt and angry for no real reason. They'd gone out of their way to be friendly, and my frustration was beginning to boil. Dawn must have noticed, because she got up and helped me up after her.

"C'mon, girl. Let's go to sleep. You've had enough culture shock for one day."

We all walked back to our half of the cabin in the moonlight. On the way, my curiosity took hold of me again and I asked Dawn who her lover in Bigstone was.

She laughed and shook her head. "Nobody."

"You have nobody?"

"Nope. Not in Bigstone, not anywhere, not any more. That's why I came home, in fact. To be alone." Then she took my hand in hers as we continued our walk. "But I might change my mind."

All kinds of thoughts raced through my mind. The men in my life flashed before me as if on parade. I thought of Dawn, and how much I liked her. And I thought about how nothing would make me go to bed with her, much less any other woman.

"What was she like?" I asked suddenly, curiosity getting the better of me. "Your first lover, I mean."

"Heather?"

I nodded.

"Heather." Even in the great outdoors, with crickets doing their best to distract us, Dawn spoke that name in a mixture of awe and venom, sweetness and steel.

"You wouldn't imagine someone named Heather could be full of fire and passion, real crazy and disturbed, now would you?"

"What's in a name, anyway?" I asked, trying to be glib.

"Heather was the complete opposite of me, that's what I liked about her, I suppose, because there wasn't much I liked about myself, that's for sure. She was wild and reckless and self-assured."

"That's how I always think of you, Dawn."

"Dawn and Dusk. Opposites attracted like fire and rain. Both stoking and fanning the fire . . . and finally choking the flames. And each other," she sobbed dramatically. "A real love-hate relationship," she went on with a tight smile. "It lasted almost a year and felt like forever. When it was good, it felt like paradise, and when it was bad, and it was often bad, it felt like hell. How's that for a cliche? But that's the way it was, something out of the worst kind of novels. Anyway, once it got really bad, I don't know who I hated more, her or me. But finally I had more hate in me than love, and by the time she left me I thought I'd never want to go through anything like that ever again. I just wanted to be alone."

I didn't know what to say, so I just nodded.

"She was my first and only love, Rosie. I can't go through this kind of turmoil again."

"Things change," I said vaguely. I thought of my own love affairs, and their sudden endings; the feeling of loss.

17

"I came back to Bigstone because I thought there, for sure, I'd be able to forget, to live alone and apart with no hassles. But then, maybe I was wrong. I sometimes have this wild desire to fall in love, share my life with someone."

"Too many movies," I tried to laugh it off.

"Maybe not enough," she countered. She sighed and took my hand. "I love you, Rosie, you know that."

"Like a sister?"

"Any way you want it, Rosie."

She looked vulnerable, then, and much smaller than ever before. I had an impulse to kiss her, to hug her and make her feel better, as sisters do, but I refrained. I didn't want her to get the wrong impression, and maybe I didn't want to get any ideas myself.

"Listen, Dawn . . ."

"Forget it. Just a thought. I'll make sure nobody hassles you here, okay? Not even me."

She laughed, but suddenly I wasn't sure I could really trust her any more.

CHAPTER THREE

That night, I had a hard time falling asleep. I thought of Bigstone, of my family and friends and lovers. Why was life so crazy? Why did every door open to a roomful of mirrors?

I don't suppose anything in my life prepared me for this kind of music festival. I mean, I always dreamed of being an adventurer, going around the world looking for treasures — exotic things, strange and different things. But I never left Bigstone, except to go shopping in Fairville or to a carnival or rodeo show in Newton. I had my dreams, of course, but there wasn't really an opportunity to carry them out.

I thought again how much I'd like to leave Bigstone, leave home, be independent like Dawn. I wondered what she was dreaming about, lying in the bunk bed across from me. And suddenly I thought of my high school graduation three years before, and how I lost my virginity.

As it turned out, Wayne liked "it" so much, and I liked him enough, that we met a few more times in the back seat of that powder-blue Ford that summer. Then he was off to college and I got a job as a filing clerk at the local silverplating factory.

By the time Dawn came back to town two years later, most of our classmates had left, for one reason or another. Bigstone has little to offer anyone with an ounce of ambition. The guys who stayed behind mostly worked where their folks did, and the girls had babies to look after.

As for me, I was just lazy. I kept meaning to leave but never got around to it.

Well actually, I almost did leave, once.

Someone had opened a fancy club in town. Not a bar, exactly, but something a bit classy, a place with a bit of style. It didn't last long, of course, but while it did, I hung out there quite a lot. I liked the music especially, a sort of danceable jazz that melted me from the inside.

One evening I was sitting there with the regular bunch, smoking and watching out for their drinking and having a nice time chatting about nothing special, when this new guy walked in.

This was it. I could feel it. My guy. My heart raced.

Helen, at the bar, was sizing him up and I knew that if I didn't make a quick move there would be no point in making any move at all. So I got up and walked over, hardly believing it was me doing it.

"I'm Rosie," I introduced myself. I was aware of the fact that I had a new blouse on and probably looked as good as I could without mirrors.

He stared at me in silence.

I'm told I have a beautiful speaking voice and I used it to advantage, but my words took on a questioning tone as his steel blue eyes focused on me. He was tall and bearded and smelled real good.

"You look new, I mean I've never seen you here before, maybe I can . . . you know . . . introduce you around?" I went on gamely.

"B36," he said at last.

"I beg your pardon?"

"I said B36. That's your bra size, ain't it?"

He was right.

It turned out that he was working at the foundation factory and had learned to size women's undergarments pretty accurately at a glance.

We danced together that night, and within a week I'd moved in with him. He lived on the edge of town in a rundown barn he'd fixed up. He had a great stereo and played the guitar like a professional. He told me he'd been in a working band once. Why he left he never said, and I never really asked.

My parents put on the pressure for us to marry, although it didn't take much to persuade me on that score. I daydreamed all the time at work about our future together—we had vague plans to go to Memphis or Nashville and make him a star. But the dream ended one day when he unexpectedly left town and never returned.

I was so devastated, I thought I'd die. But I got over him.

A couple of months later Dawn returned to Bigstone and I was laughing again.

When I woke up the next morning, I was alone. Dawn left me a note explaining they had gone off to breakfast without me. She also left a detailed map of how to get to the dining area.

When I got there I was in for a shock. I never saw so many women in one place before. All kinds of women: young and old, short and tall, fat and thin; women who looked like men, and women who looked like cover girls, and women who looked like nothing I'd ever seen before. They looked friendly, they looked happy, and none of them looked at me.

Not that I wanted anyone to look at me. It's just that I thought I looked different, and that they'd stop in their tracks and make me feel like an outsider. Then I laughed to myself: here were thousands of women who would definitely be considered outsiders in the outside world . . . and I was afraid of being considered an outsider by them.

I must have laughed out loud, because the next thing I knew Dawn was at my side, asking: "What's so funny?"

I couldn't explain, so I changed the subject—my foremost talent. "I overslept," I said as I filled the plate she handed me with enough breakfast food for a week. "Have you been up long?"

"I've swum to Cambodia and back."

Seeing my puzzled expression, she chuckled. "Just kidding. Isn't it great to be in the mountains and have a beach, too?"

"Anything's an improvement over Bigstone."

We sat on the grass and ate silently for a while. I tried very hard to avert my eyes, but I couldn't help noticing the amazing variety of breasts. Some were gorgeous, but even the ordinary ones looked special.

And I never saw obese women look so good before. When I was in school, the fat and overdeveloped girls used to hide themselves in the locker room as if they were ashamed of their bodies. But here, these big women had a way of carrying their bodies like trophies.

"Here," Dawn said, thrusting a booklet in my hand. "It's the festival program, so you'll have an idea of what's going on. At least on the surface," she added, laughing again. "There's a lot more around here than meets the eye."

"You have a lot of imagination, you know that?"

"So do you," she said, getting up. "So do you."

"Where are you going?" I asked, getting up also.

"To rinse the dishes and sign up for a work shift."

"Why? I thought this was vacation."

"It is. But just once, we gotta help out," Dawn explained as we rinsed the dishes at an outdoor tub. "Do you want to help in the kitchen, or at the concession stand, or with day care, or what?"

"Those are my options?"

"More or less. You can always volunteer for guard patrol or garbage duty."

"I think I'll help with the children."

"Sounds good. Maybe we can volunteer together?"

We did. We signed up for the next evening, which meant we'd be missing some of the featured entertainment, but I was beginning to think that I might need a break from all the excitement by then.

Meg and Cathy joined us then and suggested that they show me "the lay of the land," so we all walked over to the crafts areas, which looked more festive than the biggest fair in Newton. There were glass works, oils, pottery of all kinds, wood carvings and paper cuts, jewelry and beadwork, and lots of stuff I'd never seen or heard of before: things that had to do with the Goddess, as Dawn put it.

"Who's she?"

"Who knows?" Meg answered.

"Who cares?" Dawn countered.

"Like God, you know, only female," Cathy explained.

"What denomination?" I asked.

"Witch," Cathy replied with finality. "A wise witch. Don't let anyone hit you with that other baloney. The Witch Goddess has no religion, she is a universal spirit that can be awakened in each woman."

"Amen," Meg chortled.

I dropped the subject. Religion never interested me.

Of all the things on display, I liked the political stuff, the buttons and cards and decals, the best. I didn't understand them all, but of the ones I did my favorite was "A woman's place is in the house . . . and the Senate." Dawn bought the button for me and pinned it to my blouse.

"Welcome to the real world," she intoned solemnly. "A world where women rule. At least, themselves!"

"A world without closets?"

"You've got it," she said, and kissed me on the cheek.

It was a platonic kiss, but I felt flushed.

"It's hot. I'm going to the cabin to get my bathing suit."

"What's wrong with ours, Rosie?" Cathy asked in mock concern. "Are we out of step with fashion or something?"

"I'd really feel better with a bathing suit," I said lamely.

"Lay off her, you guys, give her a break," Dawn put in, coming to my rescue once again.

We started walking and Dawn said she'd accompany me back to the cabin. She was moody, and we didn't say much of anything when suddenly she exclaimed: "I hate it when they put on the pressure. It's like everybody's gotta be different in the same way."

"And you'd rather be different your own way, right?"

"Damn right!" she laughed.

For a minute, we said nothing.

"Let's walk by the lake," Dawn suggested at last, and we did.

CHAPTER FOUR

That first day of the festival was a day to remember. There were workshops in several places at once dealing with issues that made sense to me—like: women and the economy, women and power; and issues that did not—like: sex and the single lesbian. Best of all, there was a workshop on meditation, something I'd heard about but never had the opportunity to learn.

I thought I'd start with that. Dawn opted for a massage.

"I need a touch of TLC," she said with a grin as we parted. "To put me back in touch with the environment, and all that."

I was aware once again that she was speaking in code, unlike her Bigstone ways, which were direct and logical.

"What's tender loving care got to do with ecology, with whaling, and flood control?" I asked.

"We're talking environment, not ecology," she explained patiently. "You know, the parts of the world we interact with, like people and places and the stars."

"Don't tell me you're into this parapsychology and astrology and channeling and all that weird stuff Oprah Winfrey's always bringing up on her show," I said, adding to myself, You're queerer than I thought, Dawn!

She had always seemed earthy and, well, normal to me, and here she was going on and on about strange and silly things like "aura" and "karma" to make her point.

When I left her a few minutes later, I still didn't get it.

So imagine my surprise when I found out that "meditation" wasn't a relaxation technique but a "whole new way of approaching the world," as our workshop leader, Moonglow, put it. Honestly, at first I thought I'd come to the wrong place, but then I started to relax and listen, and it was a real eye-opener.

"First of all, sisters, we have to learn to breathe: to inhale deeply and exhale with delight," Moonglow began.

"You may think you know how to breathe properly. After all, you've been doing it all your life. But unless you become aware of the way you breathe, you may well pollute your system with the poisons of patriarchy. Think about it. Every day, men are putting toxic wastes into our streams and rivers, into the sacred bosom of the Earth, into the air around us, into our foods and into our water supply."

I admit, I'd never really thought about it that way.

"So, you ask: What is the solution? The solution is to be aware, to come to a point of meditation which is really a point of mediation between our wonderful Goddess selves and the true spiritual sources all around us. We must tap strength from them rather than from the so-called real world. Our task, sisters, is to take back the four basic elements — the air, the water, the fire and the earth — back from the boys!"

We began the workshop by introducing ourselves. Of the twenty women in the group, I was the only one with a name that didn't sound like it was made up by some writer for a book.

Some of the names I remember were: Crescent, Ishtar, Tiger, and Aurora. Some had initials only, like K.C., while others had foreign names like Natasha and Rhavindra. All of a sudden, Rosie was an unusual name.

After the introductions, we held hands in a circle while Moonglow said something in a language I didn't understand, in a way that sounded almost like singing, but not quite. Finally, she began teaching us how to "breathe purely," as she put it.

"Touch the Earth Mother with your toes, touch the Earth bosom with your heels, sweet sisters. Feel the soul of the Earth sigh beneath you as you stand with your feet slightly apart, shoulder-width. Just relax—that's it!— and let the goddess course through your beautiful lesbian bodies like an orgasm."

It was hard to relax.

The next stage was to place our hands together in front of us, as if in prayer. Then we were to lift our hands up to the "solar sky" as we inhaled the "invigorating rays of the Sun Sister" into our lungs. This was all right, and after a few attempts I managed to do it with my hands still together.

"Good," Moonglow encouraged us. She had a habit of mingling among us and touching us to emphasize her point. "Now, you must exhale very slowly as you circle with your body back to the Earth Mother, the source of our spiritual splendor."

By peeking at the others, I figured out that she wanted us to bend over. It was still hard to relax, but anyway I actually began to enjoy myself. I always liked sports, and this active kind of meditation seemed more my speed than the meditations I'd read about before, where people stare at plants or candles and say a foreign syllable over and over again.

"This is a YoniYoga meditation," Moonglow said just then, as if reading my mind. "We meditate with our whole body and soul, as a form of communication—communion, really!—with the Earth Goddess. This is an ancient form of woman-to-woman worship that has been lost for too many centuries, but now that we are able to practice our devotion to ourselves, to each other, and to the Goddess once again, it has become a more powerful tool of liberation than ever before."

She taught us several breathing exercises to go along with some basic movements, and I must admit that, despite the jargon, I learned quite a lot. I vowed to go down to the lake that evening to practice, and to continue doing the exercises every day before and after work when I got back to Bigstone.

Tiger, a small woman of about thirty-five with a shaved head who seemed never to shave anywhere else, waited for me after the workshop.

"What'd you think?"

"It was all right," I said.

"She's the greatest, a real hag. I go to her retreat sometimes when I'm in California."

"Where you from?" I asked. It sounded like she wanted some conversation, though I wasn't sure I could have anything in common with this woman.

"Here and there," she replied. Then she laughed. "Mostly, there. I haven't had a real home since I left my husband and kids two years ago."

"That must have been a tough decision," I said, maneuvering us towards the lake, my favorite spot.

"Not really. He's okay, but sort of wimpy. Too good to be true and yet somehow real. I was lucky, he's a good father so I don't have to worry about the kids."

"Don't you miss them?" I asked incredulously.

"Not for a minute," she said, lighting a cigarette and offering me one, which I accepted even though I hated the brand. "I never wanted children in the first place, but it seemed to be part of the package. Then I found out that I wasn't the only woman who was attracted to women."

"Dawn was telling me that ten percent of women are lesbians and that means, I guess, that there must be quite a few of them around," I said, trying to be nice.

"Yes, and isn't it wonderful?" Tiger went on with what I thought was unbecoming enthusiasm. "We don't have to be lonely any more."

I figured this was as good a time as any to put things straight.

"I'm not a lesbian," I explained. "I came here with a friend and a couple of her friends. For the music," I added.

She gave me a quizzical look, then went on. "You'll like Clarissa. My lover. She was also straight when we met. What a trip! Her boyfriend chased us with a shotgun at one point, he was really crazy about her and maybe crazy about everything. He kept saying over and over again how he could handle her running off with a man, but not with a woman. His masculinity was on the line, you see, and he felt like someone had socked him with a stone-filled glove. If he wasn't such a jerk, I'd feel sorry for him."

"I like men," I said, rallying to the defence.

"That's all right, you'll get over it."

She maneuvered us away from the lake and into a long cabin that was filled with rows of benches, equipment for sound control, and a raised stage full of microphones and amplifiers. I noticed a stocky woman with red frizzy hair springing from a bandanna sitting in a corner by herself, making strange gestures with her hands and fingers. I wondered what was wrong with her.

"Clarissa!" Tiger bellowed, running to the woman and hugging her from behind. "Have I missed you, honey! I want you to meet this woman here, Rosie. She was at the meditation workshop this morning."

We shook hands. Her grip was firmer than I'd expected.

"Clarissa's the signer for the day stage," Tiger explained.

I looked around. "Which signs?"

They looked at each other and then roared with laughter. "Not a sign maker," Tiger finally managed to say. "She interprets for the hearing impaired."

"Say what?"

"I translate the words of songs for those who can't hear," Clarissa put in. "ASL—American Sign Language—is a real language, like English or Spanish, and so there's no reason for those women who can't hear the songs not to be able to enjoy their message, at least."

"Not to mention the high of being surrounded by hundreds and thousands of other lesbians," Tiger added.

"I'm for equal opportunity, by all means," I said.

Just then a couple of women came in with guitar cases. One of them went over to Clarissa and handed her a small notebook.

"Hi. We're the Toklas Twins. You must be the signer. We'll be singing the first two songs from here and then a Ferron song, we haven't decided which one yet for sure but you probably know them all anyway, right? Thanks."

And she was off.

Clarissa made an international sign of frustration and then Tiger was massaging Clarissa's head and saying softly: "Don't be upset, baby. They have no idea what it's like. It's not their fault."

While Clarissa sighed, the Toklas Twins took out their guitars and started to tune up. A slim black woman wearing an African wraparound came in, sipping a soda. She turned on the sound system. It squeaked.

"What's going on?" I asked.

"Clarissa's fed up with the way everybody treats signers," Tiger replied. "These singers think it's like signers are . . . monodrones from the United Nations, for heaven's sake. They come in five minutes before they're scheduled to go on, hand her a crumpled piece of paper with illegible scribbles, and then expect her to just adlib along brilliantly as they sing!"

I noticed that Tiger had a tendency to talk in exclamation points.

"It's disgusting and I'm sick of it," Clarissa put in.

"Relax, honey, just relax," Tiger said soothingly, still massaging Clarissa's head with slow, deliberate strokes. "It's unfair, it's terrible, but it's not their fault. They've probably never had a signer before and they don't realize what it all involves!"

"What does it involve?" I blurted.

Clarissa sniffled, but then her eyes cleared as she spoke. "ASL is an art form, almost. It's a very evocative language which can sometimes become . . . a ballet for hands, when a good signer interprets a good concert where there's a lot of good energy from the audience. It's really beautiful. But most singers don't appreciate us very much and they think it's just a cute bit of staging to highlight their own show. I can't stand it any more."

"You'll be fine, honey. Just relax."

And then Calypso walked in.

I was totally unprepared for that vision again. I mean, I'd seen lots of beautiful women before but even the handsomest guy I ever met had never evoked such an incredibly spontaneous physical rush in me before. I felt my cheeks flush and my heart beat so fast that I had to inhale to keep from blacking out.

I sat down.

"Now take Calypso," Tiger said, waving her over to where we were. "A real pro. She sent her cassette with the words typed up for Clarissa to learn months in advance. You'll love her."

That, I thought, was the problem.

Calypso put down her guitar and came over. "Hi there," she said. "I only hope we'll have a bit of a crowd, and that one of the organizers will maybe peek in. Highly unlikely."

"Why?" I heard myself asking in a weak voice.

"Because we're, like, the illegitimate daughters of lesbian culture. The organizers give us a chance to perform, but that's all. They're not there for us, giving us a hand and welcoming those of us who're really good to get more recognition, which means getting into the professional women's circuit."

"If you're good, you'll make it anyway, won't you?"

"I forget. This is your first time," she said lightly, but her blue eyes turned to steel. "Lucky you. Still naive, still idealistic, still blind as a one-eyed bat. Good to see you, anyway," she said and went to the stage to do her sound check.

"Don't let her give you a hard time, Rosie. She's rumored to have a heart of gold under that iron exterior."

31

"Though you'll have to check it out for yourself, 'cause so far she's only shown another metal . . . mettle . . ."

Clarissa groaned. "I hate puns."

"Love me, love my buns . . . puns, I mean!" Tiger teased.

Then they hugged and kissed, and I decided it was time to move on.

As I moved up front, I noticed that others were trickling in as well. Again, I couldn't help but notice how diverse these women were, and yet how ordinary. Somehow, I had expected lesbians to be look-alike men without facial hair, but in fact many of them could have "passed" as teachers, housewives, factory workers, and secretaries— any kind of women—even in Bigstone. And that's what they probably were, too: ordinary women leading ordinary lives under extraordinary circumstances.

By this time, I was beginning to adjust to the notion that these women were interested in women rather than in men, but it was still a bit unsettling to see white-haired women necking in public. Somehow, I'd never associated older people with sex.

I was hoping to catch Calypso's eyes. She ignored me. But before I could get too hurt, I realized that she was ignoring everyone except the woman working the sound system from the back.

"Give me less echo on this mike, Samantha," she was saying.

I couldn't take my eyes off her as she moved on the stage in search of the perfect set-up. She wore a silky gray blouse and stylish white pants. She was barefooted, a silver chain tied around her ankle. She was so breathtakingly beautiful I was sure all the other women in the room would stop and stare, too, but it didn't take me long to realize that I had very little competition in the groupie department.

By the time the show began, I'd counted maybe thirty women scattered around the large cabin. Samantha announced that two of the scheduled acts hadn't shown up, so there remained Calypso, the Toklas Twins, and a trio from somewhere in Alabama.

The trio played a classical piece by a woman called Fanny something-or-other who died a long time ago in Europe. It sounded okay, surprisingly, considering I never really got into that kind of music.

The Toklas Twins were next. They weren't very good, but I liked looking at Clarissa as she did those funny things with her hands. At times, her whole body was in motion.

Then it was Calypso's turn to sing, and I was torn between curiosity and despair. What if she turned out to be as bad as the two singers before her? I wasn't sure I could handle a chink in that perfect armor.

As it turned out, I had nothing to worry about. She was very good.

"Hi there," she began, caressing the audience with her smile. "Music is very important to me, and I'm happy to share with you here today some of the music I've written over the last couple of years." She re-tuned her guitar as she spoke. I wondered if she was as nervous as I was. "I agree with Holly Near, who sang to us last night, that the personal is political."

Some women interrupted her by clapping and hooting.

"Who you are and who you love . . . hey! That's what it's all about, right? These are the decisions that really matter. We're proud to be lesbians—that's why we're here at this festival—but we're also proud to be caring individuals for whom everything that happens on this planet matters.

"We care about pollution, about nuclear holocaust, about poverty and about racism, classism, and ageism. But most of all, we care about each other."

The women whistled and hooted again. A noisy bunch.

And then she began to sing, and it was as if she was singing about me, about my life and feelings and concerns, as if she'd met me before and cared. To give you an idea, here are the two verses I memorized:

33

She works each day from eight to four
No-one knockin' at her door
Spends her days at the factory
Her nights in front of that TV
But in her heart she knows there's more
She hears them talkin' on the floor

> They say: union . . . union . . . union
> Join the union, join your hands
> United workers can make a stand
> Tell them that you're proud to be
> An organized woman in your company

She goes to work in a skirt and halter
Every man whistles and hollers
They like her just the way she is
Big in the bosom and small on brains
But in her heart there beats a drum
Stronger and stronger every time they hum

> The word union . . . union . . . union
> Join the union, join your hands
> United workers can make a stand
> Tell them that you're proud to be
> An organized woman in your company

She sang a few more numbers, but that first song kept playing over and over in my head, like a hit parade tune. For such an angelic looking woman, she sang in a deep, throaty voice that was a bit rough around the edges.

After the show, everyone dispersed, but I found myself lingering behind for a chance to spend a couple of minutes alone with her. I told myself that I was merely being friendly, but I knew even then that there was more to it than that. It scared me a bit that I might be attracted to a woman, but then I figured it was just natural curiosity.

There was a strange fragrance in the room, like an exotic perfume. Or maybe it was the heat. For a long time, Calypso didn't even notice me. She unplugged all the gadgets from her guitar, then placed it in its black case and secured the clasps. She did everything gracefully, and this takes time. When she was ready to leave, she finally noticed me.

"Rosie?"

I nodded.

"What'd you think?"

"I liked that song. About the union."

"Well, thanks. I like it too."

I couldn't think of a thing to say.

She waited a moment for me to say something anyway, then gave up on me and left. In a second, I ran out after her. I had no idea what, if anything, I wanted to say to her, but I did have the idea that if I let her walk away, I'd never see her again.

"Are you here alone?" I puffed.

She smiled. "Alone? With thousands of women all over the place?"

"I mean . . . are you here with someone special?"

"Everyone's special," she replied casually, "especially if she's a woman.

"You've had many?"

"My share. And you?"

"A few." And then I added quickly, "Men. I've slept with a few men. I'm not a lesbian, you see. I'm just here with a friend of mine, Dawn, and a couple of her friends."

"Scary, isn't it?"

For a moment, I sensed the makings of an empathic friendship. But then I noticed that she was smiling broadly. "You're teasing me, aren't you?"

"And you're setting yourself up for it, Rosie. Watch out." After a brief silence, she added: "Look. I'm a free woman. If you want to lose your virginity with a woman, let me know. But remember, dykes can be hazardous to your health. Lesbian sex can be habit-forming."

"What an awful thing to say!"

"That's right. Honesty has a bitter edge to it sometimes."

I ran off, enraged.

I had a lot of thinking—and unthinking—to do.

CHAPTER FIVE

I noticed that everyone was streaming in the direction of the dining area, so I followed the crowd. And then all of a sudden, in the middle of that sea of women, the realization finally hit me that I didn't know anybody at the festival but Dawn, and that I hadn't seen her since breakfast. I wondered if the massage had helped to improve her bluesy mood, and wondered whether I should be actively worrying about her.

Then Tiger was at my side, half running. "Come join us," she offered. "You look so alone!"

The "us" referred to a group of women dressed in leather. Clarissa wasn't there. Apparently, she was considered a staff member and ate apart from the "festies," as Tiger called us. I felt totally out of my element.

The group looked like a tight-knit unit, but two women broke away from the others and joined Tiger and me while the others remained behind, laughing loudly from time to time.

"She don't look like a biker," said the one wearing a thick leather choker and a chain around her waist.

"Not much of a slave, either," the other one commented. She had huge studs running up and down her tight jeans.

"Don't mind them," Tiger said calmly as we waited in line for the food. "They're okay once they let you get to know them, but don't hold your breath. Took me a while, and I had the best bike in town at the time. A huge Japanese Mama that carved up the highway and really tore into the dirt, too. But Clarissa hates bikes, unfortunately." She smiled. "We all make choices."

"You mean compromises," the chain gang woman put in.

"Don't bug me, Bo. Here, meet Rosie. Rosie, this is Bo, and this is George—whatever you do, never call her Georgie, 'cause she's picked up a trick or two working in a very tough institution! She may not look it, but she's an expert in martial arts."

"You were in the army?" I asked in wonder.

"Marines," Bo corrected solemnly.

"Wow!" I was impressed.

"Hang low, Bo," George said, scooping up some beans and piling them high on a large Mexican pancake, or whatever they call it south of the border.

"She's teasing you, Rosie," Tiger explained. "The martial arts have nothing to do with the army, it's karate and judo and stuff like that. I guess she likes you."

"She likes everybody," George said, planting a resounding kiss on Bo's right cheek. "But her heart belongs to me."

"Lock, stock, and rifle barrel," Bo agreed, and they laughed. I didn't get it.

We went out to the grassy area to eat. It was sunny and yet not too hot, just the way I like it. I made up my mind to go swimming as soon as the food settled.

The sun must have melted their resistance, because within minutes Bo and George turned into very sweet and friendly women. I could almost imagine introducing them to my father, who loved motorcycles with a passion.

"What's so funny?" they asked suddenly, and I realized I'd been laughing out loud. I told them, and they joined my laughter.

"My Dad died when I was just a kid," said Bo, "but I have a whole bunch of pictures of him, when he was my age. He looked a lot like me, or I guess I look a lot like him—whichever. I always wanted to grow up just like him."

"My father's still alive and kicking," said George. "And believe me, he can reach far and hard! I got out of his way as soon as I could. Left home at sixteen and never looked back."

We grew silent for a while, thinking. Then I saw Dawn out of the corner of my eye and was about to wave to her when I noticed that she was with some woman I'd never seen before. They were sitting alone together, almost intimately, except that even from a distance I could tell that Dawn was crying. I wondered if I should go over and talk to her, but then Tiger changed the topic of conversation to something I could really relate to, and I got all wrapped up in my own living again.

"The question is, how can we become free of our families without losing them, without losing their love for us and our love for them, while still maintaining some independence of thought and action," Tiger began. I never heard anyone express themselves so eloquently before. "Even when we hate them, we still want their respect, you see. It's a real bind!"

"That's a lot of crap, you know that, Tiger? I hate my parents," said George. "Especially my mother. She is one first-class shrew. I can't stand her. She's weak and mean at the same time. Believe me, it's something to watch. All the time my father was beating me, and her, she never said a word. Not for her, not for me, not to anybody. I can't stand spineless people."

"Not everyone can be strong like you, Gumdrop," said Bo. Whoa, did I do a double-take on that term of endearment! "And anyway, they're miles away from us and you don't have to worry about any of it ever again."

"I don't know," I ventured. "Strength isn't just muscles. I mean, don't get me wrong, it's great to be physically strong, to be able to take care of yourself whatever the situation and all that, but pure brawn is a bit pathetic, don't you think? Like some moron from the movies, fighting his way through life and getting into trouble as often as he gets out!"

"You're talking to women who can lift their weight in iron!" Tiger laughed. "They don't like anybody putting down muscles, or putting up brains. When push comes to shove, Rosie, strong women have it all over everyone else."

"Come on, be serious. You were at the meditation workshop this morning, weren't you? I'm not putting down anybody," I said, turning to Bo and George, "but I can't believe any woman would want to play these stupid games, like war. Next thing you know, women will be going into professional boxing, too."

"And why not?"

"Because it's just blood," I said. "Senseless stupid blood."

"I have to agree with Rosie on that one," Tiger came to my defence, letting her food get cold. "Boxing's not a sport, it's pornography."

"Give me a break," George snorted.

"No, seriously. It's pornography, because the audience doesn't care about the people involved, about the fighters getting their brains knocked out with their teeth. They only care about their own immediate gratification! Some like to fight, but most just like to watch a fight, same as some like to make love, and others get off on seeing movies and magazines of how others do it. That, ladies, is pornography!"

"That, Tiger, is nothin' but preachin'," said Bo.

"You're making my food hard to swallow," George agreed.

They spent the rest of the meal grading the women around us on breasts, hair, and muscles. I ate quickly and left.

I walked over to our cabin to get my swimming suit and a towel. It was a beautiful day for a swim around the lake. I remembered that when I was younger, I used to

39

dream of swimming my way around the world. I wanted to get in the water, fast.

When I got to our side of the cabin and was about to open the door, I noticed a towel hanging from it. I wondered if some of our cabinmates had gone for a swim, and were now drying out the towel in the hot afternoon sun. I wondered again if Dawn was all right.

But as soon as I entered, I saw not only that Dawn was fine, but also that I was way out of place. A blanket was strewn out on the floor, and she was on top of it, with that other woman, making love, I guess.

My embarrassment overcame my natural curiosity. I ran out, breathing hard, and bumped into Meg and Cathy on the path.

"Having a good time?" Meg asked.

I explained my blunder, and cautioned them not to go in.

They laughed. "You mean you didn't see the towel?"

"Sure. I thought . . . "

"Oh-oh! You didn't know? A towel is a traditional sign, like a 'Do Not Disturb' in hotel rooms. It means that someone inside wants everyone else to stay definitely outside. For a while."

"Don't worry, you're not the only one who doesn't know how to read these signs," Cathy tried to comfort me. "When we first moved down to Durham — we're from Pittsburgh, originally — we went driving one afternoon and I noticed a car parked on a desolate part of the road. It had a white towel tied to its antenna, and I said to Meg that it's probably a jogger who's out running. I thought they left a towel to wipe the sweat before getting into the car, you know? But as it turned out, that's the sign for a disabled car. Isn't it funny?"

I appreciated her story, but still felt awful and flushed. "I only wanted to get my bathing suit. It's a great day for a swim."

"Well, there's always tomorrow," Meg said cheerfully,

and tugged at Cathy. "Sorry this is such a chat and run situation, but we're late for a workshop."

I sat down on the grass. I don't want to give you the impression that I was all alone: there were lots of women around all the time, several tents full of noisy females laughing and playing cassettes of music I never heard before. It was all a blur, I couldn't catch the words, but the atmosphere was friendly and even happy, like summer camp.

I took out the crumpled program from my pocket and looked at what was being offered before supper. There were, again, a lot of things going on that had nothing to do with me, with several things going on at once in different places, making the choice difficult. But finally one of the workshops, on women and music, caught my eye and I decided to check it out.

On the way to the area where the workshop was scheduled I noticed again and again how friendly the women were. Everyone I passed, whether alone or in a group, smiled as if she knew me. I didn't feel isolated any more and almost wished some of them would come and talk to me. Somehow, I didn't get the feeling at all that they were only interested in seducing me.

I was becoming relaxed, at last.

The workshop turned out to be a bit boring, but I did meet Fatma there, an Egyptian lesbian. She caught my eye at one point during the session and smiled. Afterwards, we stayed behind and talked. It turned out that she was a doctoral student at the University of Florida.

"And where are you from?" she asked.

"I'm from Bigstone."

"Bigstone? I have never heard of it."

"Not too many people have. It's three miles from the edge of nowhere in any direction."

"Sounds like you are not very happy there."

"I never really thought about it, one way or another. Where you from, Cairo?"

She laughed. "Three fingers from Cairo on the map, as we say. A small village, but my father was the head of the school in our district and he believed in educating girls as well as boys, so here I am."

"A long way from home," I said. "Do you miss it?"

"Yes," she said wistfully, then added, "And no."

An Indian woman with long black hair, dressed in a silky sari, came towards us and Fatma's eyes lit up. "This is Lena, my lover. This is Rosie, from Bigstone."

"And where is your lover?" Lena asked.

"Oh, no," I hastened to explain. "I'm not a lesbian, I'm just here with my friend Dawn and a couple of her friends."

"Who *are* lesbians," Fatma put in with a smile.

I nodded.

"We are the same, then. I understand how you feel. You see, I am the only lesbian in my social circle in Egypt, or at least that is what I think. It feels very strange to be here in America, where there is so much personal freedom. You have freedom of expression, of sexual expression, of religious and political expression . . . all kinds of freedom. I envy you Americans for that. You are very lucky."

"Funny, that's what Calypso told me the first night," I said. "That I'm lucky. But what's so lucky about being the only woman alone here?"

"That is what I was saying," Fatma said with a smile that was just a bit sad. "In my country, I feel very isolated. Different, yes? Definitely different. Everywhere, I wear a mask, a mask of being like everybody else, because who I really am is unacceptable to my society. And here, in the festival environment, where I feel so normal and have a feeling of fully belonging and being truly me, here you are, a straight American woman, and for once you are the outsider. It feels very strange, no?"

She took Lena's hand gently in hers. "Lena is from India. We met here, at the university. We are both very much afraid of what will happen when we have to go back home."

"Maybe into arranged marriages," Lena said.

"Why don't you stay here in America?" I asked the, for me, logical question.

"Because it is not so easy for us. We love our families and we have our traditions," said Lena. "America is good for us as lesbians but not so good for us otherwise."

"This is a very materialistic society," Fatma said. "It is true that in the lesbian community, there is warmth, but outside there is a lot of coldness. Not like home, where we do everything with a passion. The food, the people . . . even the weather is different. It is really true: there is no place like home."

"There is always hope," Lena added. "Maybe in future we open up, like flowers. But now we hide, we pretend. Very sad."

I told them that at any rate, they looked very beautiful together. They really did. Fatma was fairly tall, with a large frame that supported a bit more weight than is fashionable but that looked very good on her. Lena was smaller, but her body also was a bit on the fleshy side. Their faces were smooth, free of make-up, and shining with goodwill . . . Okay, I know it sounds corny, but that's really how they looked to me that first time.

We exchanged addresses. They said they loved to write and had pen pals all over the world. I wondered, as I left, what would happen to them, how they would handle their parting from each other, and their return to their family circles.

I was glad I didn't have to deal with that kind of problem.

CHAPTER SIX

A few steps later, I bumped into Meg and Cathy again. You know how it is, as soon as you're introduced to someone, you see them all over the place?

"Coast is clear, Rosie," said Meg.

"Dawn was looking for you, in fact," Cathy added.

"Thanks," I said, lighting a cigarette. "Maybe I can still get into my swimsuit before dinner. I need some exercise."

"Listen. Dawn's in a bit of a muddled state right now, so give her room. Don't crowd her with questions, okay?" said Meg.

"When you see her," Cathy put in, "keep it light and stay off the personal."

I was about to tell them that I resented this lesson in how to be the perfect friend when I caught a glimpse of Calypso walking down the path. Without thinking twice or even saying goodbye, I was off, running as fast as I could in her direction.

"Look who's here," she said coolly, walking on. "The one who's definitely not a dyke."

"I want to be your friend," I answered coolly. "I like you, I like your songs. I think you've got a lot of talent."

"How nice. My first groupie."

"You're terrible, you know that? Where I come from, the ones with the thickest armor have the thinnest skins. Funny."

She smiled. "I'm on my way home to practice. Wanna come?"

"Sure."

"Then drop that cigarette and come along," she offered.

"I'm almost done with it anyway," I hedged.

"I can't stand smoke," she said, clinching it. I ground the butt with my sandal. "Kissing someone who smokes is like licking an ash tray."

I vowed silently to quit. I'd been meaning to for years.

It turned out that Calypso didn't share a cabin or a tent with anyone, but lived in a cream-colored RV of her own. The decor was surprisingly cozy, and I wondered if this was the soft underbelly of her tough exterior.

"So you're like a turtle," I said, "carrying your house with you wherever you go."

"I like my privacy."

"I like it too. Very nice house."

She pulled the guitar out of its box and went off into another room. "I hate an audience when I'm at home."

I thought she was a bit like Miss Baxter: gruff and tough and so alone you wanted to give her shelter or warmth, or just a sense of belonging to the world. But in my experience, the more you try to reach out to them, the nastier they get.

I looked at her books and music cassettes. I think you can tell an awful lot about a person from just that, and I was growing more and more curious about this Calypso woman. I wondered what her mother called her, if they were in touch at all; if she had friends. I found it hard to believe that she went through life snubbing everyone.

There were several books on ecology, a couple of books on women's spirituality, and the complete poems of Emily Dickinson, whom I liked at school because her poems were short and in plain English. There were also slim volumes of poetry by women I never heard of, like Alice Walker and Adrienne Rich. They had strange titles like *Horses*

Make a Landscape Look More Beautiful and *A Wild Patience Has Taken Me This Far.*

I could hear Calypso from the next room. She wasn't singing, but humming. Or maybe it was something like Moonglow's chanting. Somehow, I realized that she was singing exclusively to and for herself, and I felt dejected, rejected. I was sure that she'd forgotten I was around. But then she began to sing, and I was drawn once more to that rich, deep voice and those strong lyrics that I couldn't help but feel were directed at me personally.

> Sugar, honey, the love just drips
> But, baby, when you cash those chips
> There's nothin' but heartaches in your grip
> Darling, sweetheart, butterfly,
> Suddenly the good times have passed you by
> You find that they're just words and lies
>> They reel you in every time they try
>> And leave you hanging out to dry
>> High and dry, high and low
>> Wise up, girl, it's time to go
> Woman, don't you know those lines by now?
> Written in poison so that nothing can grow
> From the dust of your passion, the sweat of your brow
> Sweet soft yearning for someone to love
> How can they fool you, only to prove
> That a sucker is born cut into the groove?
>> They reel you in every time they try . . .

The melody was as haunting as the words. I began to think of my lovers: of Randy who never wrote, of Wayne for whom I must have been a fleeting diversion, of Carl who was sweet but boring. If this was love, then Calypso was right: there was a sucker born every minute yearning for a body to touch. And then they were left high and dry with a weeping soul, totally isolated and apart from it all.

Suddenly Calypso was by my side again. For a minute, I felt as if my knees would give, I was so nervous. I wasn't sure what I feared more: being seduced or being rejected.

46

"There you have it, my philosophy of that four-letter word that makes the world go round and around in circles, ever tighter circles that make us all so dizzy we never stop to see how stupid the game really is," she said.

"I guess I have a romantic streak," I tried to put in an opinion of my own.

"Good conditioning," she said, moving into the kitchenette area. "Tea?"

"What else do you have?"

"Water."

"Okay."

"Okay tea or okay water?"

"Okay whatever you're making."

"Well, right now I feel like making love."

I sat down on the sofa, my heart beating so fast and loud that I was sure she could hear it too.

But I don't think she cared. "What the hell are you here for, Rosie? Do you get your kicks from simply watching? Don't you ever want to get involved? You feel oh so superior to us dykes, don't you? Spying on us from the wings and pushing your lesbian friend in everyone's face so they won't think you're a bigot or anything. You make me sick, Rosie, and that's a fact. Get out."

She went into the other room. What hurt me most was that I knew she couldn't care less how alone I felt.

I wept all the way back to the cabin.

I lay on the mattress and smoked. The last thing I wanted to do was stop smoking because of that bitch, that's for sure. I kept repeating to myself over and over again how much I hated her. I lit and smoked one cigarette after another until I began to cough. Then I cried again.

I had no idea why I was so upset. I knew I should have felt relieved, but somehow I wasn't relieved at all. Much as I hated Calypso and never wanted to see her again, I was starting to remember all kinds of little incidents from my past that seemed to signal a very different future. I'd been wondering how Dawn had become a lesbian, but realized I had no clue. She seemed pretty ordinary to me. I couldn't imagine how or why she'd gotten so attracted to women.

But lying on that lumpy mattress, smoking rings around my troubled head, I started to think that maybe being a lesbian wasn't so strange after all.

I remembered Miss Sawyer, the gym teacher, again. She was small and muscular, nothing like other women in town, but anyway she was very popular. She had a bell-like laugh and she laughed often. Nobody thought her odd or unattractive, and nobody understood why she never married, or even dated. I remember now that even when she left Bigstone and her mother told everyone that Miss Sawyer was sharing a house with another woman and a cat, no tongues started wagging. Maybe they were naive.

As soon as Dawn told me she was a lesbian, I realized in a flash that Miss Sawyer must have been one, too. I made a mental note now to ask Dawn about that when I saw her again.

Don't ask me how I knew, but I did know now, for certain. Maybe it was the way I'd felt every time she repositioned me on the parallel bars? And my heart pounded ominously every time I saw her unexpectedly in the general store, buying a jar of pickles or a pound of cheese. Suddenly it hit me: I saw that I must have had a crush on that Miss Sawyer.

Had I been secretly in love with her? And did that make me a lesbian too? I panicked, but then a more rational thought took over: wasn't the fact that I had slept with guys proof positive that I was okay, that I would marry and have children and be like my parents?

More than ever, I thought, Dawn and I have got to talk. And what about Dawn, anyway? Was she all right? And who was that woman making love with her, anyway?

She sure forgot about me in a hurry, I thought bitterly. A new feeling surfaced: that I was a terribly wronged woman, that my best friend dumped me as soon as she met someone who loved women as much as she did, and that the one person in the entire festival who showed some personal concern for me, isolating me from the crowd, has turned out to be a first-class bitch.

Now I was really feeling sorry for myself, really depressed and miserable. I wiped my eyes again against the damp pillow and reached for another cigarette.

The pack was empty.

That was the last straw. The whole world had suddenly turned against me, leaving me perfectly alone and friendless.

I lay back against the pillow and closed my eyes. I was very tired and hoped I'd have no trouble falling asleep. In fact, I thought, maybe I'd best sleep the whole damn festival through!

All of a sudden, I wanted nothing better than to be back in Bigstone, at work, surrounded by people and places I understood.

CHAPTER SEVEN

Dawn was standing by my bed, a worried look on her face. "You should never smoke in bed, Rosie. It's dangerous."

"I probably should never smoke, period," I replied, coughing and trying to wake up. "What time is it?"

"Eleven. Are you all right?"

"Don't worry about me." I sat up and yawned. The bulb on the porch threw some vague light into the room. "Who is she?"

"Heather."

"Oh."

"It's pretty bad. We still feel passionately about each other, loving and hating with everything we've got. I don't know what to do. I guess it'll be over again as soon as this festival ends. I'm not going back to Atlanta and she sure isn't about to move to Bigstone."

I touched her cheek. "You're a sweet kid. Why waste so much energy on something so hurtful when there are hundreds of others around to choose from?"

"Easy for you to say, you don't know what it's like."

"I've been in love," I said in indignation.

"Have you?" she asked. "Have you ever felt like there were only the two of you in the entire universe, that every time you touched each other the stars were suddenly in their perfect place and the seas were lapping stormily against the shores? Have you ever felt that you were made out of the same material, blending together, yet united

50

by invisible fibers even when apart? So much drawn to each other that nothing else in the world seemed real, that nothing else mattered? That all you could do was pretend for eight hours a day, at work, that you were like everyone else, a faceless humanoid in the crowd, while knowing full well that the only time you were really alive was when you locked the door on it all and wrapped yourself in each other?"

"Not quite that dramatic, maybe, but in love. Yes."

"Well, that's how it is with Heather. Fire and ice and earthquakes and monsoons; the good, the bad, and the ugly—and the very, very beautiful."

Dawn sat down on Meg's bed. "She likes to hurt me as well as she likes to make me happy, she likes to feel free by sleeping around, but I love her. It's like an addiction. Just when you think you're cured, you try it again and you're just as hooked as ever before. Maybe more. And you know what? Like any addiction, it feels so good when you're high that you can't imagine why you ever quit. And then you're dumped again from the heights, and you cry, and then the cycle begins all over again."

"What are you going to do?"

"I don't know. Probably nothing. It'll all end on Monday anyway."

"What does Heather feel about it?"

"I don't know. We don't talk about it. I'm not sure I want to know." She changed the subject: "Wanna go to the movies?"

I got up. "Sure. What's playing?"

"You'll like it. It's called *Desert Hearts*. Good music and an interesting story about a woman who comes to Reno for a divorce and ends up being seduced by a cowgirl."

"Great. Just what I need."

But I went.

Dawn was right. The music was good. The story was okay too, until towards the end when these two women started making love and I felt strange again. I remembered

Calypso, the bitch, telling me that I was nothing but a voyeur and, watching those love scenes, I couldn't help thinking that I was. I admit I had been curious about what women could possibly do together, but the love scenes left me even more confused than before.

The audience seemed to know the movie by heart. These women shared private jokes throughout that made me progressively puzzled. I felt like an alien, like a widow in mourning at a white wedding.

Afterwards, Dawn and I walked to the lake again. There was so much I wanted to ask! But, coward that I am, I shifted the conversation to small talk instead.

"How was that massage?" I asked.

"You wouldn't believe this, but I had a terrific body massage, fully naked, from a nun!"

"You're kidding."

She shook her head. "I swear. A nun. There are a couple of them around, in full habit."

"How strange."

"Apparently, there's a whole bunch of straight women running around. They like the music and they like feeling that they can take their clothes off without being hassled by the wolves."

"How about the sheep?" I teased.

"Come on. Has anyone really been hassling you?"

We sat down on the edge of the dock. There was a full moon above, sending dancing rays on the calm waters.

"Not really."

"What do you mean?"

"I wish I knew."

She gave me a questioning look, but kept silent. We sat for a while, relishing the peacefulness of the place. Then Dawn walked me back to the cabin before setting off in the direction of Heather's tent.

I bumped into Fatma and Lena at breakfast and joined

them for the morning. They were going to a workshop on "Minority Women and Major Issues."

At this gathering, ironically, I was the minority woman; not only because I was heterosexual and they were lesbians, but mostly because I was the only non-ethnic around. Being ordinary was, again, making me unique.

Luckily, Fatma and Lena quickly sized up my feeling and made me feel at home.

"In the end, you know, the basic issues are the same for all of us," Fatma said. "Whether we're white or black or olive-skinned, fat or thin, gay or straight, rich or poor, the threat of nuclear and ecological holocaust affects us in the same way."

"The planet is small. Big egos only get in the way," Lena put in. "And people in power have very big egos."

A woman who introduced herself as Ilya, from Santo Domingo, joined our discussion. "Imagine looking at the Earth from the moon, or from Mars," she said. "How small we look."

"And how insignificant," Bella, her lover, agreed. "If we blow our planet up, it will not affect the universe one bit."

"So what does this mean?" I asked.

"It means that we have to take care of ourselves," said Fatma. "Explain to everyone who will listen that more things unite us than divide us. That we must work for unity and harmony rather than for destruction. Because there are no winners, only losers, in this kind of game."

Just then, the three women who turned out to be the workshop leaders arrived. One was a Native American, one was black, and one was Hispanic. They spoke in a very articulate way about racism, which I never thought had anything to do with me before.

I began to realize how this world was being made ever smaller by those who conformed to the division of people by color, race, religion, and sex, and how the more anyone agreed that such divisions were okay, the more invisible the people banished from the "we" of those do-ing the dividing became.

Quite a thought-ful, right?

And my next thought was, how hypocritical and judg-mental I was, too. I mean, here I was trying to prove that I was different, not a lesbian, as if that made me better, playing the "us" and "them" game as if that was the issue.

One of the panel members mentioned Atlantis, and the Amazons, but this didn't prove to be of much comfort. Knowing that somehow, somewhere in the past, things had been better only made me feel worse. Maybe things weren't as simple as they seemed.

Then something caught my ear, and I listened with a start of recognition. "The personal is the political," the black women was saying. Where had I heard that phrase before? Calypso! "The secret of the universe is now being researched on the smallest level, in the sub-atomic genetic code, as scientists are unlocking the secrets of the DNA."

She almost lost me there, but then she went on to something I could understand: "On the person-to-person level, this means that world peace will come when peo-ple will learn to love each other. War will be around for as long as even one person hates another person, some-where. There is no substitute for love."

On that inspirational note, the workshop ended. Some of the participants hung around afterwards in small clus-ters talking, while others left in their separate directions. Fatma and Lena left also; they'd made a previous ap-pointment for a massage.

I decided this was as good a time as any to go for a swim. I couldn't believe I hadn't tested the water yet.

CHAPTER EIGHT

There was no towel on the door, and nobody inside the cabin. I lit a cigarette from the pack I'd bought on my way back, changed into my bathing suit, wrapped a beach towel around my shoulders, and went out in the direction of the lake.

"Beautiful day for a swim," Meg called out. She and Cathy were dripping cool water on the sizzling path as they walked by.

"Don't forget your sun screen," Cathy said. "It's a real scorcher."

Tiger and Clarissa, both naked, waved to me as I approached. The lake was teeming with women in various stages of attire, and mostly without. I ground out the cigarette, put the butt in the trash can by the concession stand, and joined them on the dock.

"Isn't it a beautiful day?" Tiger asked, her toes just touching the water. "I love this lake."

"When I get rich, I'll buy it for you," Clarissa promised playfully.

"And I'll buy the yacht."

They laughed and, pushing each other, fell into the water.

I put my towel down and was about to take my sandals off when Calypso came out of the water, like a mermaid. My heart beat fast and my knees seemed to give, so I sat down again quickly, breathing deeply, the way Moonglow had taught us in that meditation workshop.

I was hoping that Calypso would ignore me, but she came over immediately. When she sat down beside me on the beach towel, the water was like festive sparklers on her body; a warm pool made its way towards me on the dock.

"You look good in a bathing suit," she said.

"You look good without," I blurted out.

She gave me one of her quizzical stares. "So would you."

"Plenty of naked women going around," I said boldly, motioning grandly with my hands and putting on a voice from some movie I'd once seen. "Stick around. Maybe you'll catch one."

Suddenly, her mouth was on mine and my breathing stopped for a second, then resumed at a clipped rate. My head was swimming and my lips felt seared. Was this love?

"You still smoke," she said coolly, getting up. "What a shame."

I couldn't believe it. She was walking away from me all over again. Didn't she care? Didn't she have any feelings at all? When she sang, she seemed to be totally another person, someone warm and caring, but off-stage she was something altogether different. I couldn't stand her. I wanted her dead, I wanted never to see her again. What a hateful bitch!

And then she was back, clad in a colorful sun dress that made me think of faraway places and exotic perfumes. She was smiling and looking so beautiful my heart melted all over again; it was like instant replay, and I saw her as if for the first time. Before I could catch my breath, get back to my senses and tell her to get lost, she grabbed my hand and propelled me up, and away.

I had no idea where we were heading, and I didn't care. I was open to adventure. A minute later, we entered Calypso's creamy house-on-wheels. I remembered what Dawn had said: It'll all end on Monday anyway.

"Who taught you to kiss like that?" Calypso asked,

locking the door behind us. She handed me a toothbrush and guided me to the faucet.

"I practice in front of the mirror," I said, gargling. Then, rinsing my mouth and turning to face her, I added as casually as I could: "You're not so bad yourself. . ."

She blushed and turned her face. "I didn't mean to give you a hard time. But I really do hate cigarettes."

"Me, too. I wanted to quit yesterday, but then you made me so angry I went through more cigarettes in an afternoon than I usually do in a week!"

"Go on, blame it on me." But she was smiling, and now her smile seemed soft.

"Okay," I said, trying to be flippant as my heart lodged firmly in my throat. "It's all your fault."

She leaned over and kissed me again. I nearly fainted.

"Now what do we do?" she asked suddenly, breaking away and striding towards the kitchenette. "Want some tea?"

"Sure."

So. We were back at that proverbial Square One. I wasn't sure I was ready for the next step, but I sure wanted to know what was going on, what the game plan was. And anyway, did she want me to make all the moves?

"What kind of tea do you like?" she went on, in a voice that was disturbingly calm. "I have a whole collection of dried herbs and a couple of commercial blends."

I shrugged my sagging shoulders. "Whatever. I've never had anything like that, but I'm willing to try."

"Don't tell me you're the kind who'll try anything," she said. "Once."

"Once, yes," I said mechanically. "Sometimes twice."

"Regrets?"

"Not if I can help it," I replied with what I hoped was a smile. Where did that line come from? I was still nervous and confused, but my voice sounded clear and sure.

What a game! One thing I'd noticed about people who are nervous is that they put on a mask; they're not themselves. Here I was, playing the part of the flirt, when inside, I was shaking from fear that I'd be so convincing she'd actually believe the phony me and make a play for that me. Me, who was scared out of her wits by what was happening, though helpless to stem the tide of confused emotions making me play the flirt in the first place.

And so on.

She put the kettle on and looked around. "Would you like a piece of banana bread? Maybe some music?"

Was this for real? Could she be as nervous as I was?

I decided to sit down, and did. "You know," I changed the subject expertly, "it's funny. I came here for the music, right? But so far, all I've heard was you."

"Want your money back?"

I wanted to say, "No, just you," but I didn't think that was appropriate, so I kept quiet.

Calypso poured water into the old-fashioned kettle she'd been holding all this time and, at last, placed it on top of the small range. She rummaged in the cupboard above her haloed head and after a while extracted a few dried weeds.

"I make the best tea this side of Texas," she said with a smile that seemed almost boastful. "I picked these herbs myself, in the mountains. I love the mountains. And you, do you hike?"

I shook my head.

"Too bad. What do you do to relax? Do you have a hobby?"

I though a minute, then shook my head again. "I used to play the flute in the school band, but I quit. I like music, but I never enjoyed practicing scales and I hated all those rehearsals."

"Music is hard work," she agreed. "Like anything else when you want to do it right."

She turned to face me again just as I was wondering if I should get up and help her set the table. "So what do you do, anyway? Where are you from?"

I felt very inadequate and small, unworthy of her attention and friendship. "I'm a filing clerk," I replied, my face resolutely away from hers. "At the silverplating factory in Bigstone. That's where I live."

She sat down, not too near and yet not very far from where I was sitting. I felt almost naked in my swimming suit, and wished I had a robe to wrap around my body.

"Bigstone? Where's that? Never heard of it."

"Not much to hear." Then my voice grew feistier, and I even smiled: "It's three miles from nowhere, in every direction. Nothing to write home about, maybe, but it is home."

We laughed, and her laugh was smooth and sensuous, like her music. Our eyes locked for a moment. I had that elevator feeling again. I was wondering what I'd do if she hugged me, or kissed me, or what, when the kettle whistled.

She got up — reluctantly, I thought — turned off the water and poured it into a sea-blue ceramic teapot. She placed it on a tray along with a couple of cups and brought it over to where we were sitting.

"Do you want honey?"

"I guess. Sure."

She returned with a small jar. Opening it, she scooped out some of the golden honey absently with a teaspoon and ate it.

"This is great honey. Here, try it," she offered, guiding the teaspoon gently into my mouth.

The next thing I knew, I was having a hard time swallowing and she was licking my sticky lips.

At first, I couldn't separate the two sensations, the sweetness of the honey and the full freshness of her mouth. My head reeled, and in my imagination I was falling into a cavern padded with flowers and soft bushes and newly mown hay. I reached for her body to keep from falling. Then I felt her strong, bare arms pulling my fast-falling body towards hers. I felt her shoulders touch mine, and another wave washed upon my shores.

My senses flashed another scene across the screen of my imagination. Now, I was airborne, floating like a feather in the early-morning breeze. As my head began to clear, I could see mountains and valleys and rivulets below, cascading in and out of focus. Then, for a brief second, my head cleared completely, and out of the corner of that imaginary eye I could see two women hugging and kissing on a purple-colored sofa in a small room decked with posters, potted flowers, and plush throw rugs.

I surrendered to Calypso's lips, to her embrace. If any thought passed through my overwhelmed mind right then, it was probably that I never wanted that moment to end. My fantasy was to go through life walking down endless mountain trails with her, holding hands.

I have no idea how long we sat on that sofa, kissing and hugging and feeling wonderful, but somehow, at some point, we opened our eyes and looked at each other as if for the first time. I was really shaking now, no longer from fear but from pleasure. I was clutching her tightly, as if I were a drowning person clinging to storm-smoothed driftwood in the middle of an ocean and she was my lifesaver.

"What do we do now?" she asked softly, releasing me.

I had no idea.

"I've never had a one-night stand before," she went on, turning to me.

My face was flushed; my knees were shaking so visibly now that I hugged them to my chest for comfort.

"There must be a song about this. Some stupid song somewhere that puts this situation in perspective," she added.

I knew that she wanted me to say something, but I couldn't for the life of me speak. I went on hugging my knees in silence. And even if I had had something to say, at that point I didn't trust my voice to express it.

I wanted something to happen. I admit I wanted to go to bed with her, but I had absolutely no idea how to set it in motion.

And there was something else, too: I wanted to be seduced. I had never played any other role. I couldn't believe that Calypso, brash and breezy and utterly beautiful, was waiting for me to make that decisive move. Would we end up sitting so close and so far apart forever?

She was sitting on the sofa still, her heart-stopping body just far enough from mine to make accidental contact impossible. She drank her tea in silence, staring into the steaming liquid as if trying to make out a form in the fog. Outside, I imagined, the day was throwing shadows across the lake and the moon was preparing to make its full-blown entrance once again. The room, too, seemed to be growing colder with the receding sun.

Then, another thought hit me, and I jammed my knees securely against my face. Was she waiting for me to do something, or was she just waiting for me to leave? Was she only interested in the chase, not in the catch? Was she just a tease? The thought paralyzed me, but my head held more questions still: Could she have been making a pass at me only to drop me after I showed a glimmer of interest? Was she just like a man?

Tears streaked down my face. I didn't want to cry in front of her, especially since it would only make her feel better. I'd heard about people who actually enjoyed making other people miserable. Well, Calypso had lured me into her house and now she was probably laughing while I cried. Why wasn't she saying something, already?

"It's really very good tea," she said just then, her voice barely audible.

Great, I groaned to myself.

By now, I was convinced that I was unloved and unwanted, that as soon as my knees could support my weight again, I should leave. Her words seemed only to reinforce my perception.

Calypso: the perfect hostess. Let her drown in that brew! I had no intention of drinking that tepid herbal soup, that's for sure. I needed a real drink, and a cigarette. I needed to get out of there.

I could hear her taking a deep breath, then exhaling softly. She placed her cup on the tray and turned to face me with an earnest expression. "Look. I've been attracted to women as long as I can remember, and I've been lucky. They've been attracted to me, too. And you, Rosie, you were attracted to men and, maybe, you've also been lucky. I don't know what I'm doing with you and I wish you'd help me figure it out."

"All I know is that I'm scared," I managed to whisper.

"Me, too."

"I bet."

"Why?" she said, surprised but smiling again.

"You've been there before."

"Not with you, not here, not now," she said simply.

It was my turn to take a deep breath. Could I be lucky? Will something happen after all?

She moved closer, and the smell of her body overwhelmed my senses again, but she didn't attempt to touch me.

"I really like you, Rosie. I'd like to sleep with you. But I'm not sure that's such a good idea, because you've never done it with a woman before and I'm not sure I want the responsibility. It's a heavy scene for me, you see."

I didn't know what to say.

"I've had a lot of lovers, we had great times together, and none of us ever cared how long it lasted. We were together forever, you see. Until the end."

I was feeling her satin voice washing over me like spring rain, and I warned myself not to get trapped. This was obviously the kiss-off, clearly it was time for me to go. But when I tried to get up, my knees felt numb.

"I don't want this to be a brief encounter, Rosie, and let's face it, realistically there's no way it can be anything else. So what do we do? What do you feel about all this?"

"I think I've been had, is how I feel."

Calypso looked genuinely puzzled. "Why?"

"Why?" I repeated incredulously. Was she that insensitive? "Because you've been making a pass at me ever since that first night. You brought me here, to your home, you kissed me passionately, and now you freeze up and turn everything off!"

"Nothing's turned off," she said softly, and this time she tentatively placed an electrically-charged hand on my arm.

I wanted nothing more than to embrace her, to kiss her again and again, but I made sure that my hands stayed firmly away from hers. I had the feeling that any move I made would seem stupid and show my inexperience in the worst light.

"I like you fine, you know that. I'm just thinking of you."

"Don't think for me, okay?" I shouted, getting up. I was really angry now. "I'm twenty-one, I'm not a baby any more, okay? I know what's going on. I admit it, I've never felt like this before and it's scary. But don't tell me you're thinking of me or doing anything for me when all that's on your mind is some excuse to turn your back on me and grow icicles in front of my face, okay? I should have known better than to come here, anyway."

"I thought you wanted to come," she said defensively. Did I detect a sign of hurt in her voice?

"I did."

"So?"

"So what now? Do you want me to go, or what?"

She smiled, and suddenly she kissed me again, lightly. "Or what?"

I won't bore you with the details, but the next thing I knew we were wrestling on the floor. She was quite powerful, but after all, I hadn't hung around the boys all my life for nothing. I'd picked up a trick or two of my own. Within five minutes, I had her pinned to the floor, breathing hard.

"Aunt," she managed to say.

I laughed. I liked her sense of humor. "Aunt," I repeated. "I like that."

We stayed like that for a moment, intermittently laughing and trying to catch our breath.

I knew that this was it, this was our now-or-never moment. A movie I had seen once flashed before me: this was where the guy lets his fingers do the walking, trying at first playfully and then more and more insistently to fondle the girl's breasts.

My face felt as if I'd just stuck it in the oven with the cake, hot and flushed and dizzy. What should I do? What would bother her more, my making a move or my not making a move? And anyway, how would I go about it?

And then, in a crazy moment, I said: "B36."

"What?"

"B36. That's my bra size. Some guy once told me that right out of the blue, it was so funny."

"Well," she said, trying to raise her chest from the floor, "I hope you gave him a kick in the pants."

I blushed even redder, and decided against telling her the truth. Sometimes, honesty is not so much policy as suicide.

Changing the subject as usual, I said: "What kind of line works for you?"

"Oh, the usual," she laughed and, catching me off guard, pinned me to the carpeted floor. "Wanna see my etchings?"

I'd seen that movie, too.

"Or how about Mae West? 'Officer, is that a gun you're wearing or are you just trying to be friendly?' " I offered.

She leaned down and kissed me. A century later, she asked softly: "What if I were to tell you that we're out of gas? That we can't get out of here?"

"I'd probably get out and walk," I answered, not letting her face get too far from mine.

"That's what I was hoping you'd say."

"I saw a station about a mile down the road," I went on, in as serious a tone as I could muster. "It's raining

elephants, but what the hell? Honor comes before life, ladies, that's what my Mama used to say."

"You're kidding!"

"I am."

"Oh," she said, getting up, but her voice was hard
again. I felt as if a cold front had swooped in from the
North Pole.

"What did I say?"

"It's nothing you said. All of a sudden I remembered
Mama. May she rest, as they used to say. The only thing
Mama used to say was, 'Pass the bottle.' Sometimes, for
variety, she'd say, 'Pass the bottle, stupid.' She was very
articulate."

I didn't know what to say. I liked my mother.

"Sometimes I wonder how I ever got involved with
women, the way I hate my mother. Even now that she's
dead, I still hate her. And sometimes, I still feel guilty."

"Why guilty?" I asked, and wondered if I should go
and give her a comforting hug.

"Because I always wished she were dead, and then
when I was fifteen, she died in a freak accident and I
thought it was all my fault. They put me in therapy for a
while, and I guess it helped a bit, but every so often I still
get that feeling, that I'd better run for cover. Like something's gonna hit me unexpectedly from some shadowy
corner and I'd die, too. And sometimes I just feel like,
hey, what's the big deal, let me end it all right now and
get the suspense over with."

"You mean you've tried to kill yourself?"

"A couple of times," she said matter-of-factly.

"I love life," I blurted. It wasn't the most tactful thing
to say. I decided to get up and hold her after all. "Every
day I wake up smiling. I'm anxious to start a new day,
even though I'm not doing anything special or glamorous
with my life. I like my family, my friends, I guess I'm
happy with what I've got. Maybe I lack ambition, but I
can't even imagine wanting to kill myself."

She hugged me, and for a long time we just held each other, like sisters. I wondered briefly how Dawn was getting on with Heather, and what she'd be thinking if she could see me now.

"Why are you smiling?"

I told her.

"And what do you think, Rosie?"

"About what?"

"About this."

"Us?"

She nodded.

"I don't know. The last thing I expected to find in you was a friend," I said at last, truthfully. "I really hated your guts, you know that?"

"And now that you have me in your arms, you like my guts just fine?" she said airily, but I heard that hard, bitter edge again in her voice.

"I'm not sure what I have in my arms," I said. I don't know why, but suddenly I wasn't scared any more. In fact, I almost felt protective towards this beautiful but terribly vulnerable, fragile object masquerading as a bed of nails.

"And neither am I," she said with a sad smile, letting me go. "Will the real Rosie Malone please stand up?"

"Come on, I'm an open book," I said, sitting down on the sofa again. Calypso looked restless.

"I can't make up my mind," she said. "You seem like an earthy type, honest and fresh, but—I don't know. I guess I don't want to feel that you're just curious, that you've decided that while you're here at the festival you might as well relax and have an adventure with a lesbian."

I was painfully aware that she had touched a weak place in me. I felt awful. Maybe the thing that hurt most was how close she'd gotten to the truth. After all, I knew that the thought had crossed and double-crossed my mind: that going to bed with Calypso would be all right because I'd never see her again and nobody would ever know. I'd

66

be safe, back in the real world of Bigstone, by Monday night.

She interpreted my silence for admission, and I guess she was right. "I never go to bed with anyone who just wants a body. I want to feel that I count, that the woman's interested in me, Calypso, the whole of me."

The sun must have set at last, because the room was quite dark now except for a reflected glow from an electric light outside. Even in silhouette, she looked stunning. I knew that I was not conventionally pretty, that my body was not made for the cover of a magazine, and I wondered how I could have ever entertained the thought that she'd be interested in me.

Then, I thought again that I should quit smoking and take up some healthier pursuit and, with the nondenominational Goddess guiding my hands, I got up, took a step towards Calypso, and finally held her in my arms, kissing her hair and face and mouth as if I only had five minutes left to live. And maybe I did.

I still had no idea what to do next, so I kissed her again and she guided me back to the sofa. I thought that the next logical move was mine: to caress her breasts. But as soon as my hand reached into her dress, she froze.

"I'm sorry," I pleaded. "I shouldn't have done that."

"It was just a surprise, that's all," she said, breathing quickly in and out.

"I'm dying to sleep with you," I said. It was kiss-and-tell time. "I don't know what's happening to me, but I know I want to go to bed with you."

She gave me a searching look. Then, she kissed me, undressing me as she did so, before taking off her dress and guiding me to her bed.

CHAPTER NINE

I'm going to have an uphill struggle with this part of the story, folks, but I know I can't chicken out now and talk about the weather, or the decor of that room, or simply pull a Margaret Mitchell and tell you that I woke up happy the next morning, though that much certainly goes without saying.

I suppose there's nothing to do but give you a play-by-play, blow-by-blow account of what happened, so here goes.

Calypso was, as I noted once again, absolutely breathtaking naked. I felt my heart constrict, then race, as my eyes took in the smoothness of her skin, the firmness of her breasts, the size of her nipples, and the fullness of her thighs all at once.

I was further bombarded by another sensation: there was an intoxicating fragrance in the room, like the scent of exotic, faraway places.

"What is that smell?"

"Like it?"

"I guess."

"It's sandalwood," she said, smiling. "My sister went to India and all she got me was some incense."

She laughed but, noticing that I didn't get the joke, she explained. "You know, like the kind of things that say: 'My friend went to Alaska and all I got was this lousy T-shirt'? This is a bit overpowering, huh? Like sticks of dynamite, maybe. Blow you away."

She was right. But what really blew me away was the way my body felt electrified when her hand touched my face, then made its way slowly down to my shoulder. I thought surely physical sparks would fly all over the room, but it was probably only my charged imagination playing tricks on me.

"You're trembling," she said with a hint of wonder. Pulling me gently against her chest, she asked: "Feeling better?"

What can I say? Her fully unclothed body, beating softly against mine, felt warm and supple. On closer inspection, her nipples proved to be large and firm. There was no movie to guide me through this scene.

Suddenly, with one movement, she crushed my body against hers and wrapped her leg around mine, tripping me over the bed. As I fell, I pulled her over me.

She smelled great and I felt an urge to inhale her deeply. I did.

"What are you doing?" she asked, giggling and trying to break away. "Stop it!"

I could tell she liked it. She was ticklish, and that was something I could relate to, at last. My little brother was ticklish and I had a terrific time tormenting him. I buried my nose in her breasts, wiggling it playfully between them.

She was laughing hysterically now, in a high-pitched howl that I found as melodic as her singing.

"What are you doing?" she asked over and over again, in-between howls of laughter. I could tell that she liked it, so I went a step further and took her left knee between the fingers of my right hand and tickled it, making her truly hysterical. Finally, she reached for a pillow and threw it at me.

I grabbed the other pillow, and then we were like a couple of schoolgirls at an overnight party, except that where I grew up, we all had frilly night things, nobody was naked. And then we were running all over the small trailer, giggling, tossing and catching and avoiding each other's pillow.

And then she kissed me.

It was an even more amazing kiss than the ones before. I kissed her back, longingly, and in a minute had her below me on the sofa, my hands fondling her breasts perhaps a bit too eagerly.

"What a wild little virgin you are," she said, coming up for air. "And here I took you for the passive kind."

I stiffened beside her. Was I? For a minute, my thoughts wandered, and I reviewed the statement in my mind. With Randy, of course, I had been passive, but afterwards I certainly made sure my lovers knew that I was definitely interested. Still, it was true that every time I went to bed with a guy, it was at his initiation, although I was a very willing follower. Not your truly passive type, perhaps, but not exactly aggressive, either.

"Have I offended you?" she asked, concerned, her long hair falling around my face like those waterfalls, her hand on mine. "I didn't mean to, honestly."

I shook my head. "I'm just thinking. I've never done it with a woman before, but look at me: here I am, forward as can be, literally putting my nose in where it doesn't belong."

And then we looked at each other, tented by her hair, and started laughing with abandon, feeling totally relaxed and at ease, like old friends.

"And what a cute little nose you have," she said at last, rubbing hers against mine. "Had it long?"

"It's a recent implant, but it's taken rather well, don't you think?" I replied, kissing her.

"There's certainly no sign of rejection. Not on my part."

"So it's the nose, is it?" I asked. "I should have known."

"I have this thing about noses," she confided between short kisses. "What can you do. It takes all kinds."

"What kinds have you had?"

"That's dangerous territory," she said, "you don't really want to know." This time her kiss lingered. My head spun all over again as her tongue played with my teeth. It was a good thing I was already lying down.

Her hands now fondled my breasts and for a minute I thought I'd gone under, I was so faint. I was trembling all over, all over again.

"Tell me, how does it feel?" Calypso asked, her hands moving expertly around my buzzing breasts.

I swallowed. It was hard to breathe, let alone talk.

"Just relax, Rosie, okay? Just let yourself go and enjoy."

I couldn't relax, I was so excited. Places I never knew existed in my body were suddenly coming alive.

"How does it feel?" she repeated, nibbling at my left ear.

"Fine," I managed to whisper.

"Just fine," she asked, her hands caressing my breasts more and more urgently, her fingers teasing my nipples erect.

I brought my face towards hers and kissed her on the mouth, then let it go, confused. Was I coming on too strong?

"Now kiss me like you mean it," she told me gently, moving her lips towards mine.

I grabbed her face and gave her a hard kiss that seemed to last forever. I felt as if my whole body was on fire, blazing hot, sending sparks to choice spots all over, and then I felt the opposite reaction, too, gooseflesh.

I shivered slightly.

"It feels good, does it?" she asked, kissing me again. She took one of my hands in one of hers and guided it to her chest. "I like it, too, when my breasts are caressed," she said softly.

The heat in the room had nothing to do with summer. It felt more like what I imagine a rain forest to be, hot and wet and wild and terrific. Even our sweat smelled like perfume.

I touched her breast gingerly, not wanting to hurt her. What surprised me was the fact that it was as exciting to touch her as it was to be touched by her.

"You're a quick study," she said approvingly. "Or is this something else you've practiced in front of the mirror, like kissing? Or maybe" she added wickedly, "on yourself?"

She kissed me again, then took her mouth away from mine for a second and licked my ear.

Her mouth was like a conch shell, carrying the sound of a far-off ocean. I felt the foam, and the salt, and the cool breeze that sent another shiver down my spine. It was as if a tidal wave had come to rest against my sandy shore.

"Tell me," she whispered hoarsely. "How does it feel?"

"Calypso," I managed to say.

She switched ears, whispering: "Why don't we go back to the bedroom? It's more comfortable."

I heard her voice through a maze of webs enveloping me like a tiny wet insect. I felt faint, and yet wonderfully alive. And then the next thing I knew, I was holding her face in my hands and kissing her eyes, her nose, her cheeks, her mouth.

"You are some great kisser, you know that?" she managed to say. "Lucky boys."

"Lucky me," I said, kissing her again and again.

"Lucky us."

We were both breathing heavily now, coming up for air just long enough to stay alive for the next round of lip massage. If I had been passive in the past, that was no longer the case. I found myself wrapping my arms around Calypso's body as if she was a fragile art form, gently. I raised her from the sofa as I got up to my feet.

She did not resist.

"I love you," I said, easing us down to the shaggy carpet on the floor.

"What's this obsession of yours with love, anyway?" she asked as her lubricated lips found my breasts again.

"I don't know," I replied, kissing her hair from above. "But I love you anyway."

For a minute, she grew pensive, and her lips grew cool. Then she smiled mischievously and hugged me closer.

"I don't believe in love," she said, breathing into my ear and sending tremors down my spine again. "But isn't sex great?"

"Isn't sex love?"

"Let's not get too heavy about this, okay?" she countered with a swift slap on my buttock. "Let's just have fun."

Then her lips sucked my breasts and her hands massaged my buttocks. I felt as if someone had shot me full of arrows which were set to explode in flames upon impact. My head felt light and airy, like smoke.

Smoke! I was dying for a cigarette.

But when she touched my pubic hairs with one hand, fondled my breast with the other, and tongued my ear, I forgot every other desire I ever had. I only wondered what I could do to make her happy, too.

She must have read my mind, because she said softly: "Let's play mirror."

"Play what?"

"Play mirror. You do what you see or feel me do. Okay?"

"Sure," I said, taking in a deep breath. "Where do I start?"

"Just remember that the greatest thing about women making love with women is that we care about what our lover likes," she began, exploring the roof of my mouth with her tongue and sending seismic tremors into my brain.

My tongue licked the back of her teeth, then her inner cheeks, then her moist tongue (was this the original meaning of tongue-tied?) while I explored her pubic hairs with one hand and pressed her buttocks with the other.

As our mirror game progressed, I lost my orientation completely. I couldn't begin to tell which of us was doing what to whom. It was as if we had melted into one unit, breathing and feeling as one: one body, one mind, one soul, one woman.

"You are a quick study, honey," Calypso said. "Now let's switch, okay? You lead and I follow, so to speak. I'll be your mirror for a while."

I nodded, but I couldn't think of anything new to do.

"You don't have to be inventive," she smiled, whispering in my ear. "Just let it flow. You know?"

I kissed her squarely on the lips, and she kissed me roundly back, enveloping my tingling lips with hers. I caressed her hair and she fondled my hair in turn and then, out of turn, returned to my breasts.

"Has anyone ever told you what wonderful nipples you have?"

I blushed.

"They are," she insisted, kissing them for emphasis. "They are soft and firm, demure and outgoing all at once."

I fingered her nipples gently. "Look who's talking."

"Who's talking?" she asked, and kissed me deeply again.

We took turns at the mirror, switching so often that we soon forgot who was supposed to mirror whom. The world became one giant mirror, and everything reflected in it was beautiful, and loving, and real.

But then, just when we had become welded into one being, gossamered together with filaments of desire, Calypso got up.

I panicked and reached for her, but she was smiling. A minute later, she laid her glowing body over mine once again, and her body was more desirable to me than ever.

Now, she was facing my feet. I grew self-conscious. Did they smell? Was my skin too dry?

"For some reason, lots of people forget the feet. The feet!" she cried in triumph. "Believe me, feet are sexy, too," she said, and began to massage mine soothingly.

"If you want me to play mirror," I cautioned, "you'll have to let me sit up."

"Relax, honey. Just lie back and enjoy."

I did.

She reached over for a small bottle and oozed some scented oil onto my feet, working it into my thirsty pores. My whole body felt Calypso's fingers and thrilled with their movement. I felt as if I was in some colorful meadow, ringed by wildflowers, running joyfully, chasing butterflies, laughing and smiling and feeling like a happy child.

"This is great," I managed to say at last. This purring cat, I thought proudly of myself, was polite!

"Isn't it?" she agreed with a smile. She handed me the bottle. "Your turn."

She kept one hand on my body and turned around again, so that her feet were next to my hands without my having moved at all. Lazily, I squirted some oil on her soles and massaged them. Making her happy was making me very, very excited.

I slowly worked more and more oil onto her feet and then, on an impulse, moved further and further up along her legs. I could feel her relax and smile.

"We've unleashed a cute little sex monster here," she said gently, squeezing my legs to make me know she liked it.

I blushed anyway, and stopped just above the knees. For a minute, neither one of us moved. We breathed softly in unison and held hands. Then, Calypso got up slowly and pulled me up towards her.

"I love sexy ladies," she smiled, and kissed me so sweetly that I thought the stars had come out in the sky and the earth stood still. I was running again through the fields, through tall grass, and the smell of the flowers was making me lightheaded. I was flying.

Finally, we sank back into the carpet, cradling each other.

"This is crazy," Calypso said at last, caressing my ear. "But don't wake me up. Ever!"

We lay there for a minute longer, savoring each other's body close to our own. Then Calypso smoothed the hair from my face. "Yes. We've definitely unleashed a wild and wonderful animal."

"I feel more like a rain-soaked flower."

She kissed me. "Flower. I like that. Let this be your new name, the way some tribes let their people choose an appropriate name for themselves. Your name is Flower, now."

"Flower," I repeated. "Flower Malone."

"It has a nice ring to it, don't you think?" she agreed. "Desert flower, waiting for a drop of rain. It could make an interesting song."

I sat up on one elbow while gazing at her with so much loving that I thought my eyes would melt from longing. "Nobody ever wrote me a letter, let alone a song."

"Me, too," she replied, and I felt a note of harsh sadness in her voice all over again. "That's why I have to do it myself."

The air shifted again in that room, as if the spell was broken. The jungle was gone, replaced by the evening's shadows.

Calypso got up, pulling me with her, and went to the pantry. "I'm famished. How about you?" I nodded, hugging her from behind, not wanting to let go of her — or the feelings she had aroused — ever again. "How about an omelet?"

I said that whatever she made was fine with me.

"These are organic eggs, from chickens that run around in a big yard, not like the ones you get in the store. I brought them with me from home."

"And where is home, Calypso?" I asked, scrambling the eggs.

She shrugged her shoulders and diced some vegetables. "Any place I park my truck is home."

There were so many questions I wanted to ask! But for the moment, I was content to sit on the shaggy rug and eat alongside this angelic being, this perfect being who had just made me feel more like a woman than any man ever had.

CHAPTER TEN

I woke up with the sun. Calypso, fast asleep, was curled into a ball on the other side of the bed. I reached out to touch her, but as soon as my fingers found her bare skin, she curled up even more tightly, and groaned.

I wondered if she was having a nightmare, if I should wake her up and ask. I wanted nothing more than to hug her, but something warned me to let it go, to leave her alone, although my hands ached to touch her and my body longed for hers.

I got up and walked over to the kitchen area to make myself a cup of coffee. I needed a cigarette, but I had none with me, and anyway, I'd quit. There was no coffee anywhere, only bags and bags of strange-smelling dried leaves and flowers and pieces of bark. The refrigerator held nothing but vegetables and cheese.

I looked at the kitchen clock. It was seven in the morning. Outside, I could barely make out the sound of a bird. I decided to go for a swim.

It was obvious the women's music festival didn't exactly attract the early-riser types. There was a heavy silence all around. I wrapped my towel around me for extra warmth.

As I approached the dock, I saw that someone was already there, her body covered with several layers of clothing.

When I got closer, I recognized the woman with joy.

"Good morning!" I cried out.

Dawn turned to face me, then got up.

"What are you doing up so early?" I asked, walking towards her on the tottering wooden dock, arms outstretched for a hug. "You're on vacation, remember?"

"Where were you last night?"

I blushed.

"We were supposed to help out with day care, remember?" she went on. "I was worried sick about you, Rosie."

I had forgotten. "I'm sorry."

"You weren't there at dinner, you weren't there at the show or the dance—I asked Cathy and Meg to flush you out—and you weren't in bed, either! You really gave me a fright, you know that? Anyway," she added with a smile, hugging me like the best friend that she was, "Heather pitched in for you."

"Great. At least something good came out of it."

"I don't know. I wish I knew what the hell was going on between us, where it will all end."

I sensed at once that something was wrong. "What's up?"

"I woke up early and decided I needed a breather," Dawn replied, her voice full of sorrow. "Things are a little weird between us, Rosie. Somehow, she's decided to be jealous of you."

"Jealous of what? There's nothing between us!"

"I know. But she's funny that way. She wants complete freedom for herself, no questions asked, and then she gets paranoid about me and every woman within binocular range."

"She's crazy."

"I like her that way," Dawn said with a tight smile as we sat down on the dock together, just like that first evening. "Anyway, knowing her, I think she's just looking for an excuse. Tomorrow's Monday and she can't stand unfinished business, and everything between us is still way up in the air. I haven't made up my mind one way or the other yet, any more than she has. Hell's bells, it's difficult to make a choice when things are always see-sawing." She tried a smile on me for size. "Our ups and downs are in the pits right now." Then she gave up smiling and just turned her face away so I wouldn't catch her tears.

"Well, it can't be all that bad if you can still joke about it." I wasn't about to let her stay blue, not the way I was feeling, so happy I could almost float.

"So tell me where you were."

"Here and there," I said lightly.

"Okay, suit yourself," she said. "I'm not pushing."

Don't ask me why I didn't tell her about Calypso right then. Maybe I'm a bit superstitious, thinking that if I told her, Calypso would simply evaporate, like a magician's aide. Or maybe, if truth be told, I still wanted to preserve an exit for myself even then, some safety hatch back to the "real" world carved out for me since childhood, the world of Bigstone.

Just then, Heather ran up the dock towards Dawn, crushing her in her arms as soon as she was within grasping distance.

She was a powerfully built woman with short auburn hair arranged in tight curls around her freckled face. She didn't look any more like a lady killer than I did.

"Sweetheart," she said to Dawn, kissing her face as she spoke. "Let's not waste the day fighting. Okay?"

Dawn nodded, suddenly transformed into a radiant woman.

"And you're Rosie, right?" Heather said, turning to me. I nodded. I didn't think this was the appropriate time and place to tell them that my name was now Flower Malone.

"Dawn's positively in love with you, but that's all right with me," she went on, hugging me. "In fact, everything about her is all right with me."

Then, in a conspiratorial tone, she stage-whispered: "I'm trying to lure her away from Bigstone. Don't ask me what she sees in the place. Maybe you can talk her out of it."

"You know Dawn as well as I do. She's stubborn."

"I'm more stubborn still," she winked, hugging Dawn again.

When they kissed, I felt a passion between them that made me miss Calypso all over again. I couldn't understand what I was doing on the dock at this chilly hour, when I should be nested in her sensuous arms. I ran off without saying goodbye, but that was okay because they didn't even notice.

But when I ran back, Calypso seemed far from happy to see me, as if she had been hoping I'd melt away with the moon like some mythological creature of the night.

"Listen, I have to practice and I have a lot of things to do. Why don't you go home?" she suggested tartly.

"Home?"

"Maybe you can drop by later, in the afternoon, and we'll see what's up. Okay?"

I was determined not to cry. I never cry in public and this was not the place to start. I was so stunned, so hurt, that I could say nothing, only stare back in disbelief.

"This festival means a lot to me," she went on casually, straightening out the pillows. "I came here to launch my career, it's my big opportunity, and I'm going to grab it. Got that?"

She was dressed in very efficient clothes that left no room for doubt about her honorable intentions. She wanted to make sure I knew that what happened last night was just a mistake, something that won't happen ever again.

It felt awful.

Calypso took out her guitar and spoke to me while tuning its metallic strings. Her voice was as efficient as her clothes. "One of the producers is coming to the day stage this afternoon, and if she likes me I may get a gig on the main stage tomorrow."

Icily, I said: "And if your songs don't do it, you can always invite her over for a closer look."

She slapped me, which I expected. I slapped back her even harder.

"Remember never to pick on someone stronger than you," I advised, walking out. I closed the door behind me just as something breakable hit it.

I couldn't make up my mind what to do next. All I knew was that I didn't want anything to do with her, or with any other woman, ever again. I just wanted to go somewhere quiet and die.

I entered the cabin and crawled into bed. I decided to sleep the day off. I had had enough excitement for one day.

Maybe for a lifetime.

But sleep would not come. Instead, I replayed the night before over and over again in my mind, trying to garner clues for what I might have done wrong.

I had never made out with anyone on the first date before, and breaking that First Rule of Dating was probably my biggest mistake. On the other hand, I argued with myself, tossing and turning on that narrow mattress, Calypso certainly didn't invite me over just for a cup of tea and a chat. She wanted it, too.

Was it something I said, or failed to say? Did I misread her intentions? Did she only want a bit of flirtation, an adventure?

I was getting a headache from all this circular thinking and reminiscing. Automatically, I reached over for another cigarette, but the packet was gone. I'd smoked them all. I tried to fall asleep, but that, too, proved futile. So finally I just gave up fighting the inevitable, decided that what I really needed to cheer me up was a cigarette, and a cup of coffee, and got up.

I went out in the direction of the kitchen. On the way, I bumped into Bo and George and bummed a cigarette.

"You look like you've been run over by a truck," Bo said, lighting my cigarette with a pink lighter.

"That's pretty much what happened to me, all right," I said, inhaling deeply.

"Want to talk about it?" George offered.

I shook my head. I didn't wanted to talk or think about it ever again. I thanked them and went in search of some coffee.

I spotted Fatma and Lena setting out the coffee urns for breakfast. They waved. I returned their greeting and walked on a bit faster. The cigarette tasted like sawdust. I ground it on the floor, picked up the butt and threw it in the trash can by the coffee urns. Even in my distressed state, I didn't want to litter.

"You look tired," Lena said with concern, pouring me a cup. "You take milk?"

I shook my head. "I'll take it neat, thanks."

"Are you all right?" Fatma asked with concern.

The next thing I knew, I was crying, and running back to the cabin for refuge. Fatma ran out after me, but I soon outdistanced her and she went back to the dining area while I slunk into bed.

I cried for a long time, then finally fell asleep from sheer exhaustion. In my dreams, I was a flower, and the waterfall was carrying me away towards an unknown darkness.

Dawn was at my side when I woke up, a look of concern on her suntanned face. "What's going on, Rosie?"

"Huh?"

"What's happening to you, girl? Are you all right?"

I rubbed my face and got up. "What time is it?"

She told me. I had been asleep for three hours. I suppressed a yawn and went to the bathroom.

"I'm worried about you, Rosie. Maybe it wasn't such a hot idea to bring you to this festival after all. You're been really funny ever since we got here."

"Don't go feeling responsible for me," I shouted as I brushed my teeth. "I'm a big girl now."

But she was still looking unconvinced when I came back, somewhat refreshed. "I'm damn serious, Rosie. You've been acting very strange here. If you were a lesbian, I'd think maybe you'd met someone and were starting an affair, but as it is I don't know what to think."

"You're pretty warm, actually," I said, sitting on Meg's mattress. "I have met someone. But it didn't work out."

She sat down across from me and took my hands in hers. I never realized how large and protective they were. "I don't know what to say," she began tentatively, massaging my palms.

"Neither do I," I tried to smile.

And then I was crying all over again. I cried for all the times I'd ever been hurt in my life, for all the times I'd been misunderstood, stood up, shook up and alone; for all the times I couldn't make myself understood; for all the times I'd been depressed, repressed, made to feel small; for all the dreams I never had the guts to pursue; for all the frustrations and anger I had ever experienced; and for all the times I hadn't had the space to cry.

When I stopped crying, I told her what had happened: how I had been smitten by Calypso, how she had lured me to her place, and how she had turned a cold shoulder to me when it was all over. I even told her how I was thoroughly confused and very, very unhappy.

Dawn said nothing. She just listened. Her reassuring hands never left mine, nor did her face ever betray judgement. Even when I finally stopped talking and started crying again, she sat with me patiently, never uttering a word of censure or advice.

"I'm so glad to have a friend like you, Dawn," I sniffled. "What would I have ever done without you?"

"For one thing, you'd never have gotten into this situation in the first place," she said, smiling ruefully.

"You know as well as I do that I don't regret what happened, only that it's over," I said. "So. What was it like for you?"

"Heather was my first lover," Dawn began, her voice taking on a sober tone. "I think I knew for years that I was attracted to women, and anyway I certainly knew that men didn't turn me on, but I never did anything about it. I probably thought I was a pervert, a one-of-a-kind freak. I don't know. I was pretty much a loner in the Lone-Star state, for obvious reasons."

Her hands suddenly felt cold, and I rubbed them. "It was only when I finally cleared out and came to Atlanta that I began to realize that there were plenty of other women like me, all kinds of women. I can't begin to tell you how liberating it felt to discover that I was not alone, that in fact lesbians come in all kinds of shapes and sizes and points of view, from all kinds of backgrounds.

"The bad part was that I also discovered that many lesbians, and also gay men, lead double lives, blending into the so-called outside world. They only let the real them show through in the safety of their small circle of friends and lovers. It's a very small and somewhat incestuous world in our community. Maybe in San Francisco and places like that it's different, because there are lots of us—I mean, me—around. Maybe in some places not everyone and her great-aunt knows who was involved with whom before, and for how long, and so on and so forth, blah blah blah. Who the hell cares, anyway?"

"You mean it bothers you that Heather's been around?"

"Been?" she snorted. "She's a regular butterfly. I keep promising myself never to see her again, I know she's all wrong for me, that she's just playing with me, nothing serious, but then I see her again and it's like lighting, I'm struck all over again. I must be crazy."

"I know what you mean."

We sat like that for a while, holding hands and feeling friendly. I wondered what Calypso was doing. I wondered if she was thinking of me at all.

"I guess it's time to go to lunch," Dawn suggested, getting up and pulling me up along with her. "You could use some food."

I nodded. "I'm hungry, all right."

And then her lips were on mine, and mine were on hers, and my heart was racing out of control.

"I'm sorry," she said all too soon, breaking away. "I don't know what got into me. Forget it, I'm sorry."

"It's all right," I said, trying to shrug it off. What the hell was going on? Was I irreversibly a lesbian from the moment I slept with just one woman? Would I be attracted only to women—all women!—from this moment on? I wasn't sure this was what I wanted. I had some thinking to do. Alone.

"I shouldn't have done that."

"It's not your fault."

She ran a hesitant hand through her unruly hair. "You reap what you sow."

"Then those were some wild oats," I said, smiling it off. "I've always liked you the best, and I still do."

But Dawn didn't look very pleased when we went out into the throbbing noon-day sun.

CHAPTER ELEVEN

I felt energized after lunch and wanted finally to go for a swim. But the sky was becoming overcast at an alarming rate, which isn't so usual for the South, but it meant swimming was out of the question for the time being. I still hoped that the sky would clear up sufficiently for me to jump in the lake at least once before we left.

Meanwhile, I decided to go to a workshop on "Lesbian Love, Lesbian Lore." Dawn and Heather opted for the day stage, and I suspected that Dawn wanted a closer look at Calypso.

Like me, everyone attending the workshop had a wind breaker on, and sneakers or boots. It was growing cooler outside, and increasingly more humid.

The woman who led the workshop was called Lavender Lizzie. She told us that she was from Oregon and shared a farm with a herd of cows, a barnful of chickens, a dozen goats, a donkey, ten horses, and several other "dykes."

"Wherever we live, whatever we do, we all share a common lesbian culture," she began, "so it's important to find out what it's all about. As far as I'm concerned, a woman is a lesbian when she loves women: physically, emotionally, and spiritually.

"There are many forms of relationships, and a commitment to a life-partnership is not the only valid expression of love between two women, any more than it is between two men — or between a woman and a man."

Some women interrupted her by whistling and boo-ing. "Please, sisters!" Lavender Lizzie countered, her hands held spread above her head. "Remember that if it weren't for the love between men and women, we wouldn't be here today."

I remembered my parents, and reddened. If they could see their offspring now, maybe they'd wish they hadn't loved each other quite that much, or that often . . .

"Nobody should feel guilty because she's not inter-ested in commitment—there's that 'c' word again—" The women were hooting now, laughing. The ice was bro-ken; we liked this double-L lady. "There's nothing wrong with women who are into casual contacts, or want a string of short but passionate affairs, or even no love at all in their life at this time.

"Let's face it, when we grew up, for the most part we had our parents as our most immediate example of life-partnerships. If our parents were divorced, or abusive, or controlling of each other, we grew up to rely more and more on folklore, television, and so on for our fantasies of true love, because the culture into which we were born placed an enormous emphasis on love."

The women clapped. They were clearly enjoying this woman's rap. I bet it also helped that she was very, very cute. She was tall and commanding, dressed in a lavender halter and soft, white cotton pants. I couldn't help but notice that her belly button was turned out like a pinkish coil.

"According to the American Heritage Dictionary," she went on in her strong, accentless voice, "love—I quote— is: 1. An intense affectionate concern for another person; 2. An intense sexual desire for another person; 3. A be-loved person. Often used as a term of endearment; 4. A strong fondness or enthusiasm for something. That's the dictionary definition of love, and even the dictionary rec-ognizes that there's nothing intrinsically heterosexual about love.

"But interestingly enough, love is not a real hot topic in feminist theory, believe it or not. Book after book published by feminists for the past twenty years ignores love or derides it. That's pretty funny, right? Because to my mind, that's what lesbianism is all about!"

Again, as if on cue, the women applauded wildly.

"So where are we? What do we have left, if love is a no-no? Sex, of course. Plenty of references to sex all over the place, and why not? Sex can be wonderful. Am I right?" The women were wild again. "Of course I'm right! But why the bad press about love? Any ideas?"

A woman shouted that "maybe love is just a four-letter word" while someone else groaned loudly; another tried to explain the differences away in Freudian terms, but she was quickly crushed to silence by voices of dissent.

"Okay, okay. It's true. Commercialized love is just so many feelies pre-programmed into a machine: put in a coin, press a button and bingo — you're . . . what? in love/loved/loveable/loving, right, or your money back. It's true. Under these conditions, it's easy to see how love loses not only meaning, but hope.

"Love becomes a sterile concept rooted in Madison Avenue myths. That's why Holly Near says that all her songs are political, even the love songs — maybe especially the love songs! I agree with her that we must be wary of love songs, even hers: they can be manipulative. Love songs, written to express a very deep emotion for a specific person, can create a superficial sensation in a perfect stranger. Of course, that's the strength of a good love song, too: it puts into words something that we've intuited but couldn't fully put into words. And after all, that's what this festival is all about!"

The women clapped again. Here was something they could really relate to on a very personal level. As for me, I kept on thinking of Calypso, and my face became flushed in direct proportion to my increasing heart rate.

"There's more to love than Hollywood or pornography. Isn't it time we reclaimed our right to love the women we love with a wholehearted caring, with compassion and with passion and, yes, with a sense of fun? Love is powerful. It calls for some kind of commitment. And commitment is something pretty new to our community as a political issue. It's PC to think 'c'!"

The women cheered. Then one woman shouted: "JC was PC, JC was gay! JC was cool, he was okay!" and another woman chimed in: "Celibates of the world, unite!" while everyone hooted and clapped, laughing wholeheartedly.

"If there is any lesbian message of love in my book, it is this: in order to embark on any relationship, even friendship, between women-loving-women, we must first of all feel comfortable about ourselves. That means that before we can fully like and relate to the wonderful women all around us, and I understand that we're talking about 4000 sexy lesbians—"

She was interrupted again by hoots and whistles. The woman sitting to my right had a book written by Lavender Lizzie, called "Loving Lesbians." I toyed with the idea of buying a copy.

"I swear! 4000 hot, red-blooded lesbians on the land and you're wasting time here at my workshop?" she went on, and the women laughed and clapped, and everyone was happy and relaxed.

"Anyway, if you're here, you might as well get the full Gospel of Saint Lizzie! We must address the homophobia within us, not just the homophobia that's around us." Homophobia? I'd never heard the word before. "And I'm sure you won't be surprised to learn that homophobia isn't in the American Heritage Dictionary, or Webster's, or any other." I felt a bit better, although I had no idea what homophobia was.

"But then, we all know that our society is full of paradoxes, don't we ladies?" They hooted assent. "Even if we all know that homophobia is rampant, that there is a vicious hatred of gays and lesbians in this great home of the braves, it's not even defined yet! And it's important that we define it, and love, too, because words have power. Words, too, can kill.

"Let's face it: just because we're lesbians doesn't automatically make us perfect people, though of course we come pretty close . . ." The audience went wild again. "When we meet a Lavender Lady—and we sure can spot one a mile away, can't we?—we tend to rush over and fall in lust, knowing instantaneously that THIS is IT, for how can it be otherwise? But at the same time, we tend to be judgmental, too—just like everyone else, right? Let's face it, women aren't necessarily sisters.

"Very simply, what I'm saying is that to reach out, we must first of all reach within; to feel for others, we must first of all feel for ourselves. Lesbian culture is new, and lesbian culture is evolving. It is a culture of caring, of sharing; it is there for us."

I was hanging on to Lavender Lizzie's every word by now.

"Self-hatred is not a good place from which to relate to another woman in a caring, respectful, concerned, and joyous way. It is important for our well-being as people generally and as lesbians specifically to own up to our prejudices and to come out singing. And coming out is what it's all about. Coming out to ourselves, accepting ourselves for and as who we are, truly, without masks or mannerisms; coming out to our friends and to our family— coming out not from guilt or shame, but from a need to share all of who we are with those closest to us; and coming out to our environment, to the people whose lives intersect ours in the store, on the bus, at City Hall, at work, at play, at the ball park . . .

"Coming out is scary, but coming out is, finally, the only way to accept ourselves from within and, thereafter, to reach out and touch other women-loving-women like us. Ultimately, the process is both satisfying and empowering; it is like growing up—accepting our image as well as our vision, accepting our being as well as our becoming, and accepting our strengths as well as our sorrows.

"So let's hug the wonderful women around us and chant together, as I suggest in my book—" and here she smiled broadly, and she looked almost as dazzling as Calypso, "and which is available from your friendly book booth in the crafts area. I'd be happy to sign it for you there after this workshop."

I wondered if I'd have the nerve to actually buy the book and get it autographed by this dazzling woman.

"Before we disperse, though, let's all chant together this mantra I've made up for us as we get stronger. If you've read the book, you know the words: Loving Our Selves, Loving Lesbians; Loving Our Selves, Loving Lesbians."

It was quite interesting how everyone chanted together, and how I was swept to join the crowd. It made me feel like I belonged, like I was no longer a phony. And it made me long for Calypso, and vow never to see her, in a circle game of mixed, bewildering emotions.

After the workshop, I asked the woman who had sat on my right, who told me her name was Malibu, how she rated Lavender Lizzie's book. She raved about it.

"This woman is very smart. She's got common sense and lots of experience counseling lesbians from coast to coast. Would you believe she was once a nun?"

I said I didn't.

"Well, she was. It's a fact. For almost ten years! I can't figure it out, you know? I mean, ten years is a long time. But the main thing is, she got out and then she came out and now she spends half the time on the farm and half the time on the road giving lectures."

"Sounds like a crusade."

"Yeah. I guess it is. She sure has a mission. Isn't she great? Her lover is something, too," Malibu went on, this time in a more conspiratorial tone. "She was once a Mormon, you know, sharing a husband with six other wives? Except she found she liked the wives better than the husband."

I said I could believe that. By then, I'd figured out the appropriate responses to such news.

"You bet! Anyway, he finally kicked her out. I guess he grew jealous of the way the wives liked her more than they liked him, you know? So she took her daughter and just traveled around from commune to commune until she came to the farm in Oregon where Lavender Lizzie was. She was actually almost a hermit in those days, no longer a nun but still a virgin, you know? But when she saw Annie, I guess it was love at first sight and they've been together ever since."

"Sounds like a great love story."

"Isn't it?"

"So how long have they been together?"

"About five years."

"Is that, like, a long time?" I hazarded.

Malibu nodded emphatically. "My longest relationship lasted a year and a half."

The weather turned nastier. The winds began to howl and rain was imminent. We looked at each other and, without talking, went in search of shelter together. Just then, the first roar of thunder sounded, and a bolt of lightning lit the horizon. We ran towards the dining room.

Safely inside, sitting at a table, we continued our conversation over a cup of coffee.

Without her wind breaker, Malibu looked even younger than me. "I can't believe how young you are!" I blurted.

She smiled, and her face looked even more like a teenager's. "I'm old enough to vote, and I've been a lesbian ever since I can remember."

"You don't look it."

"Isn't it great? No hassles."

"What do you mean, no hassles? Aren't guys all over you?"

"Nope. The word is out that I don't put out. They leave me alone. So do the girls, of course, but then I like older women." She smiled again. "You alone?"

I blushed. "I'm not exactly looking, and I certainly don't feel old."

"Oh? I'm curious." She reached into her wind breaker and pulled out a pack of cigarettes. "Want one?" she offered, preparing to light one for herself.

"No, thanks. I've quit."

The words sounded forced, but I tried to give them some meaning.

"In that case," she said, putting the smokes back, "I'll do without, too. I admire you. I've tried a million times, but I always go back."

I didn't feel like such a hero.

"How long have you been smoke-free?" she asked.

"Since yesterday."

She burst out laughing, until she coughed. "Excuse me. You just looked like such a survivor!"

I laughed, too. "So ask me how long I've been a lesbian."

"All right." And in the voice of a radio interviewer, she asked: "How long have you been a lesbian?"

"Since yesterday!" I replied, and we laughed hysterically again. "You bet I look like a survivor!"

"It must be exciting, anyway. I remember my first time, I was fifteen and my piano teacher left town. I didn't shed a tear, I hated the piano, you know? I mean, I only did it for my parents, who are really sweet. So then one day my mother tells me that she's found this new teacher just around the corner, practically, and takes me over.

"Well, it wasn't thunder and lightning, not with my mother scrutinizing the scene, but there was this sense of instant recognition, you know? This was definitely like nothing I'd ever experienced kissing Nora in the bathroom in school, let me tell you. I knew I was graduating to the big time when she winked at me as soon as my mother's back was turned.

"Let me tell you, Flower, the longest week in my life was waiting for the next piano lesson, you know? I practiced forever, I really got those runs down pat. My mother sent me over alone because it was so close and she had better things to do than chaperon a fifteen-year-old to a piano lesson, you know?"

We laughed. I really liked this fresh-faced kid.

"Whoa. Believe it or not, not only did I lose my virginity, I got to be really good on the piano that year, too. It was an amazing experience. But then she was accepted to grad school a thousand miles away and it was over. We knew it wasn't exactly a rational kind of affair, but it was terrific while it lasted and I still can't get over how lucky I was."

She clearly expected me to contribute to the conversation in kind, but I had a hard time being so casual about something that was still recent, painful, and unresolved.

"You don't have to tell me anything," she said at last, breaking the silence after another roll of thunder shook the roof. "It took me a while to be able to talk about it, you know."

"I'm sorry."

"Don't worry about it." She sipped her coffee, then said: "I find it amazing to see so many women, so many different kinds of women, all in one place and they're all lesbians like me! I think it's cool, you know? It really blows my mind."

"Yeah."

"Seriously. Show some enthusiasm, will you? We're talking 4000 lusty lesbians here, 4000 women with 4000 stories, can you just picture it? Totally out lesbians and lesbians who've never left the closet before. Lesbians who've been with the same woman for twenty years and lesbians who change women like underwear. If they wear underwear," she added, and we laughed again. "Lesbians who are into leather and lesbians who are into lace. Butches and femmes and androgynous dykes. Lesbians with cats and lesbians with dogs. Lesbians who live in rented rooms and lesbians who have their own condos. Lesbians who share and lesbians who hoard. All kinds of lesbians!"

"Lesbians who like women and lesbians who like themselves," I added bitterly. "Lesbians who like to tease and lesbians who like to hurt."

Malibu placed a nail-bitten hand on mine. Her green eyes grew large with concern. "Whoever deflowered Flower was a bitchy bee, you know? But there are plenty of others in the field."

I looked into her eyes and saw the invitation, loud and clear. There was no disappearing ink in that message. It would be so easy to just drift over to wherever she was and sleep my blues away . . . with her . . . But I had a feeling that while that would solve one problem, it would only create another in its place.

"I still love that bitch bee," I said softly.

She nodded her head slowly. "I see. A real bee sting."

"Yeah. How does the song go? 'I got it bad and that ain't good.' That's how I feel."

"We gotta get out of the masochism rut, all of us. Lesbians are always getting shit and asking for more, you know?" Then she smiled brilliantly again and got up. "l gotta go. I have a date."

I sat in that hard chair another hour, just thinking, while the thunder and lightning chased each other across the rain-soaked skies.

CHAPTER TWELVE

While my mind drew circles around every detail of the past twenty-four hours and the coffee soured in my styrofoam cup, the dining area filled with women eager to escape the storm. Their happy cacophony as they invaded the room lent a measure of inevitability to my own muddled thoughts.

Five women, whom I'd seen at Lavender Lizzie's workshop, sat down at "my" table and, with a small friendly nod that indicated they'd seen me and it would be all the same to them if I joined their conversation or stayed out of it, immediately began to talk. I admit, it was hard not to eavesdrop.

"Can you just picture it?" a medium-sized heavy-set woman with short curly hair began. "My best friend was in love with my husband, and I figured, all right, let her come into bed with us, what the hell? And the next thing I knew, I wasn't jealous of her, I was jealous of him! I really freaked out, I mean, I'd known Sandy for years and years and I'd never felt like that about her before. Going to bed together was never on the agenda before, right? She came to visit us and was feeling these real sex vibes, right, and automatically assumed she was reacting to Jimmy, but in fact she was getting the hots for me."

"So what happened?" asked a slim black woman who wore a wide-brimmed red hat that matched her lipstick.

"What happened is that all three of us had a wild orgy, is what happened. Nobody wanted to let anybody else know what they thought was really happening, in case it wasn't really happening after all, right? I mean, none of us had any background for this sort of thing. We were such silly . . . innocents!"

"And so the three of you established a ménage à trois and lived happily ever after, is that it?" asked a pimply-faced young woman who wore crimson shorts and a turquoise sweatshirt that said "I Am One, Too." One what? I wondered, but it was rude to ask and anyway I wanted to hear the answer to the other question.

"I wish. No, there was no follow-up, only a let-down. She left the next day and Jimmy and I resumed our quote-unquote normal life until I met Helen at a PTA meeting."

She looked doe-eyed at the woman sitting next to me, and I moved my head involuntarily in that direction also. Helen was a small, big-framed woman with salt-and-pepper hair and clothes that, though casual and sporty, obviously didn't come off a rack.

"Tell us your coming-out story, Helen," said a woman of about thirty who looked like a hippie, a long brown braid wrapped around her well-scrubbed face.

"Belinda wasn't my first lover, either," Helen said in a voice that matched her clothes: unassuming but refined. "I don't know if I should be telling you this, I find it hard to believe myself, but my first lover was my father's secretary."

The women laughed and whistled, making Helen a bit nervous and withdrawn. But she rallied shortly and went on: "Her name was Felicity. She wasn't very old, but she's the kind who was never young, either. The kind we always thought of as spinstery, and mousy. The kind who never went on dates and never bothered with fashion. You know the type: dependable, boring, bespectacled . . ."

"And then you took her glasses off one afternoon just after the last file was firmly placed in its drawer and voilà! She was transformed into Grace Kelly!" the pimply-faced

97

young woman with no color coordination breathed expectantly.

"The truth is, she really wasn't beautiful at all, in fact she was a bit on the heavy side and had more facial hair than I ever thought I could stand on a woman, but she had the most amazing sense of the absurd, she was intelligent and warm and super-fun to be with."

"I adore hairy women," the hippie-looking woman announced.

Helen gave her a side-long look. "What happened was that I was home from college that summer and had just broken up with Rodney, my fiance since high school. The details are boring, but of course in the end we did get married and it was a strange marriage indeed. The usual story."

"So what happened?" the slim black woman prodded, placing a long brown cigarette between her red lips.

"I went into the office a couple of times a week to help with the paperwork, I was so bored. Little by little, I became friends with Felicity, she was a lot of fun and I really liked her. We began spending more and more time together after work, going to the movies and to museums and even on Sunday picnics and stuff. It was a pleasure to be with her, she was very sweet and much more knowledgeable than anyone in my set."

"I bet," the pimply-faced young woman interjected. Helen's lover gave her a light kick under the table.

"At this point, she means sophisticated, not sexy," the slim black woman said, lighting her cigarette. Then, mistaking my look of addicted craving for a look of desire, she winked at me. I went back to staring at my coffee, not without blushing.

"To make a long story short, one day after a movie she suggested that we go to a bar on the way home, and it was an all-woman bar, and she came out to me. She was very nervous, I suppose she expected me to run away without finishing my daiquiri or something, but instead I found myself kissing her very lightly on the lips."

Her voice trailed off as her memories took over.

"And then she kissed you, and you kissed her again, and then you went to her apartment, and you made love, and then your father found out, and there was a scandal, and your father disinherited you, and . . . have I missed anything?" the pimply-faced young woman asked.

"Actually, not quite," Helen said coolly. "You see, she wasn't living alone, she lived with her ailing mother, and so we couldn't go to her place at all. Nor to mine, obviously."

"So what happened?" the slim black woman asked, inhaling deeply. I wished for a crazy moment that I were the cigarette in her lips, and the thought made me blush once more.

Helen took a small breath and surveyed the women at our table. "Plastic. I took her to a hotel and we charged it."

The pimply-faced young woman hooted. "I bet. The sparks flew, there was so much electricity. You charged it, all right, the place must have needed a fire brigade when you got through!"

"And then the summer was over, and we parted, but it was the best summer of my life. Until I met you," she added, turning to face her lover with a sheepish grin.

"Okay, okay. Moving right along, we have Nougat—I swear, that was her name—" the pimply-faced woman began her story.

"No! Nougat Trader?" the hippie asked.

The pimply-faced young woman nodded, a bit stunned.

"What a small world! I met her at the March on Washington, we ended up rooming with the same dyke in Georgetown. She's quite a character."

"Yes. Well."

"So what happened?" the slim black woman asked, catching my eye again.

"I was hitchhiking around Europe before college, and then at this youth hostel in Wales I literally bumped into her at breakfast. She made a sudden movement or something, and her coffee was all over my toast and my jam was on her scrambled eggs, and our clothes were a mess. We apologized, and wiped each other with napkins, you know, it was the obvious thing to do, but then suddenly I realized that she was really turning me on. So I tried to tell her, no, stop, it's all right, I'll be okay, don't fuss, and all the while we're standing there in the middle of the dining hall and, like, touching each other through the napkins, it was so bizarre."

"Nougat's a bit crazy, all right," the hippie verified.

"So she suggested that we go back to the dorm and change our clothes, and so we went back, and by then everyone was downstairs eating so she grabbed me and kissed me and it was . . . what can I say? It was great! The last thing we wanted to do was go out anywhere, so then Nougat suggested that we lay low and keep out of sight when they lock up for the day. You know, youth hostels are closed between ten in the morning and five in the afternoon. So we did, and we spent that whole day making love. It was wonderful but then it turned out that she was involved with someone already and her lover was coming down from Scotland that evening by train and, well, it was pretty messy. I wouldn't have minded sharing her, but she had other plans and that was that. I was a diversion for her, and she was a revelation for me."

"That's a great line," the hippie remarked approvingly.

"Isn't it?" the slim black woman said, crushing the half-smoked cigarette and placing the stub in a little box. "My first time, I admit, wasn't anything like that. Unlike this weather, which is all thunder and lightning," she added as the thunder rolled across the sky again and we saw a blinding flash of lightning through the windows.

"I'd been sexually active since puberty and never could figure out what the fuss was all about," she went on. "Then I got pregnant and miscarried and then I got pregnant again and this time I got an abortion and then I got to thinking that I'm not getting such a fair shake from this sex business. The guys got the fun and the gals got the pain, as I saw it.

"So then I decided it was time for a little change of scene and moved to Miami. Big town, big bucks, whew! But one day this woman came up to me at work and started to talk union. I tell you, union was the last thing on my mind, but she really managed to put some zap in the old rap and got me convinced that I should at least go to the meeting. So I did. And there she was, in her jeans and checkered shirt, and she looked kind of cute but I reminded myself that she was probably just another do-good white college kid trying to ease her conscience or get a medal or something. So what happened? She gives a speech that just about knocks me over, it's got that much fire and sincere anger in it. I went over to her afterwards, sort of shy, 'cause at that point I hadn't even finished high school and I wasn't a great talker anyway, and told her I liked her speech. And she tells me to wait till after everyone goes out and would I like to come to her place for a drink. Whoa! Sure, why not? So I did, and it was pretty bad whiskey, but we talked and talked and all of a sudden I had a friend and we were talking and it was great. But nothing happened that night, or that summer, either."

"Another sizzling summer," Helen said with a smile.

"Believe it! But she gave me her address and she wrote, and I wrote, and then she came for a visit, and I went up to Orlando once to visit her, and we became closer and closer, and I was feeling all kinds of strange feelings, I wasn't interested in guys all of a sudden, all that mattered was her. I was very, very confused, let me tell you, so finally I wrote her about it. I guess it was like a love letter. She didn't call or write for a whole week and I thought I blew it, I turned her off with too much honesty—you know how it is—but then she showed up, she looked terrible, and told me that she had done a lot of thinking and that maybe she loved me, too, and what do people do about it?

"She was really freaked out, 'cause she was a believer and this was a major sin, we were perverts, the whole bit. But anyway we ended up making love that night, or trying to, we weren't really sure what you were supposed to do or anything."

"Sort of feeling your way around," the pimply-faced young woman said. "How cute."

The slim black woman took a deep breath and now her voice was shaking. "Like I said, the first time wasn't anything to write home about. But it got better."

"I bet."

"For the next couple of months, we saw each other a lot and fought a lot and she was paranoid a lot and she wanted to break it off a lot and then we'd make love again a lot and it was a crazy, crazy cycle."

"So what happened?" the hippie asked.

The slim black woman lowered her eyes. "She killed herself."

We were all stunned into silence. I felt like touching her hand, like saying something comforting, but then I didn't know her and anyway, she had four friends to console her.

I listened to the thunder, and thought how strange it was that I was feeling a kinship with these women, that I was identifying with their lives so quickly, even though I wasn't quite sure if this was the real me coming out or just a passing passion that would grow fainter and fainter with time.

And then a couple of women from the next table went over to the piano and played four-handed versions of some old-fashioned blues. I liked their music, but they were replaced all too soon by someone who belted out satirical songs I couldn't even begin to understand.

The laughter in the room made me feel isolated again, and lonely. I missed the physical presence of the woman who had made me the happiest and, at the same time, the most miserable woman on earth. Overnight.

The laughter was quickly replaced by silence as a giant of a woman approached the microphone. She was certainly the strangest looking woman I had seen so far at the festival, and I wondered how I could have failed to see someone so conspicuous before, since I'd really walked around so much and thought I'd seen everyone on the land at one time or another.

She was tanned and strong. Despite her size, her muscles did not hide her femininity and her pretty face shone with health. Her neck, long and regal, sported a thick silver choker studded with rhinestones. One arm was tattooed with a butterfly, the other with what looked like an ax.

She wore a loose-fitting sleeveless dress that ended way above her knees, showing off her muscled legs. She wasn't wearing a bra, and a pair of erect nipples pierced the thin white material. She wore criss-crossed sandals.

"How'd y'all like this here sound and light show we've arranged especially for you?" she asked, and her voice was amazingly soft and sensuous.

I wondered who she was.

The women went wild, hooting and clapping with vigor. I leaned over and asked the woman closest to me who the woman with the microphone was.

"You mean you've never seen Myra Huntress before?" the woman hissed back in surprise. "She's one of the producers."

Immediately, I visualized Calypso and Myra Huntress making love and felt even more awful than before. I had no chance at all. If this was the competition, it was definitely over for me.

"Seriously, it's a pain in the asshole to have nothing better to do than contemplate our navels, cute as they are. Of course, we could have decided to double the fee now that we've turned the place into a floating motel, because as you know lesbian dens are a seller's market these days. You better believe it! But then we remembered that this is the last night of the festival, and that maybe you've had enough sex for a while. Am I right? Am I right, ladies? Have you all had enough?"

The women cheered wildly and made a few off-color remarks that I tried to forget as soon as I heard.

"So we've been calling the weatherwoman—I swear, she has the cutest li'l voice this side of Appalachia, but don't go callin' that number now, y'hear, 'cause I heard her first—and Lulu Mae told me to tell all you broads in here that the storm is only passin' through. All right?" The women stomped on the floor and otherwise whistled their approval loudly. "All right! So let's all sing together now, the hit song of summer."

For twenty solid minutes, several hundred grown women sang "Rain, rain, go away" at the tops of their voices while a few dozen did a "No Rain Dance" around Myra Huntress.

And then the rain stopped, and everyone headed for the doors. I sat on in stunned solitude for another minute, then walked out also.

If singing could stop the rain, maybe swimming would stop my tears.

CHAPTER THIRTEEN

I went to the cabin for a shower and a change of clothes. It was cool and damp, but the sky was clear. I decided to go to the show that night and hear some good music at last, maybe even stay for the dance and have a good time. Life was too short.

I fished for the alarm clock under Meg's mattress and discovered that it was nearly six o'clock. As soon as I took my clothes off and headed for the shower with my toiletries, Meg and Cathy emerged, dripping, giggling and rubbing each other with one towel. "Hi, Rosie. Haven't seen you in ages. Having a good time?"

"Okay."

"There's still some hot water left, but hurry. There will probably be a rush shortly. So get going!" they advised.

They played tag all the way to the mattress, and I ducked into the shower to muffle their joy. The last thing I needed was a further reminder of how much I missed Calypso.

Oh, don't worry: of course I still hated her! Wouldn't you? But I longed for her, too. She had cast a spell which was still very, very strong.

I chose my clothes carefully, just in case I bumped into Calypso again. I wore my best pair of jeans and a beautiful blouse that I once bought for too much money when I was too happy to care. I put on a pair of silver earrings and a silver chain with my birthstone on it around my neck.

Meg whistled and Cathy ogled, too. I passed inspection.

"Go kill 'em, sugar."

I left the cabin feeling better than I thought I'd be able to feel for years.

I introduced Tiger, Bo, and George to Fatma and Lena over supper. They took off on a discussion of the weather and I scanned the room for Malibu. If she was free, maybe she could save the first dance for me, just to get me started.

But when I finally spotted her, I realized at once that she would be the last one I'd want to approach that evening, and that I would do well to steer clear of her even if our paths did cross, because she was sitting on Heather's knees. They were kissing with such passion and abandon that it seemed to me that the air around them was sizzling.

I gulped down my food and went out in search of Dawn.

The air was cool and fresh, full of vague promises of new and better things to come. A hazy moon was rising lazily in the southern sky, and I had the feeling that it was smiling. I was feeling energized, renewed, and invigorated. Almost, happy. Maybe I didn't have it so bad after all. Maybe I'd survive.

I spotted Dawn on the edge of the wooden dock, as I knew I would. She was crying, and I guess I expected that, too. I went over to console her, not knowing exactly what to say, but feeling like I ought to say something, as her friend.

She gave me a look of utter despair when I sat down beside her, but she did not resist my hand as it covered hers in its grasp. I had the feeling that she was, in her sad way, glad to see me.

We sat in silence for a while. Somewhere, a sound check was going on. I could hear laughing women walking by the shoreline. It was amazing how all you saw were happy women. I wondered where the others went when they needed to cry.

"Rosie, you're the only friend I have in this whole wide world," she finally sniffled.

"And you're my best friend, too," I said, with feeling.

She touched my cheek, then cried again. I sat patiently by her side, waiting for the tears to trickle and then stop. It was rather dark, the moon was rising very slowly and at any rate it was only half full.

"What's up, Dawn?" I asked at last. "What's eating you?"

"Don't worry," she sniffled. "I'll be all right."

"How do you expect me not to worry when my best friend's crying her eyes out?" I said, placing my arm tentatively around her shoulders.

"You don't want to know about it," she said, averting her swollen eyes.

"C'mon, Dawn. Just tell me what's bugging you, okay?"

She did. And it made me sick to my stomach.

"My father raped me, Rosie," she began in a subdued voice.

She told me then how her father had abused her almost every day until she graduated from high school. "I never really had a father before, so I assumed that fathers always had sex with their daughters. How was I to know? Who was there to tell me?"

"That's awful!"

When Dawn decided that she wanted to go to college, Tom Wilson put his foot down and forbade her to leave home. She was scared, but she was determined.

She ran away, finally coming to rest in Atlanta because she couldn't think of a bigger place to run to, or one farther away. There, she worked as a waitress while taking night classes at the community college. She didn't have a special hobby, or talent, but she did have ambition. She wanted an education and she wanted to be comfortably independent as soon as possible.

"Oh, Dawn, how awful for you!" I cried out, hugging her and placing my lips on her tears.

I really didn't know what to say. Rape is something that happens once in a while even in Bigstone, and I suppose there are those who come home drunk and beat up their wives and children, but incest is a very different matter, something nobody ever really talks about, or wants to believe.

"I wish I'd known," I added gently. "I wish I'd been able to give you the help and support you needed."

"You're a terrific person, you know that?" She turned to me and tried to smile. "A real friend. I mean it."

Then she wiped her tears on her shirtsleeves. "A while later," she went on, "I met Heather. I thought she saved my life. She was so loving and understanding, so strong and so wise, and fun—" her voice broke off with a sob. "I love Heather, I love you, what am I going to do?"

"You're going to go to bed and forget us both," I said with a smile. "You're certainly not in any shape to make rational decisions right now. Sleep it off."

She nodded her head and looked sad. "You're probably right."

She squeezed my hand, then said: "I know I need help. I went to a support group for incest survivors this afternoon, for the first time in my life."

"A support group?"

"You know, women who've gone through the same experience. Incest. Hell, in Bigstone I feel like I'm the only one in the world who's ever been abused by her father! But here, I got to meet other women in my situation. We talked, and we cried, and we gave each other the strength to go on, I mean somehow it looks possible to get over it all, maybe in my own lifetime. Like, it's okay to be angry and to feel cheated, and to feel good and healthy about yourself, too, at the same time. It gives me strength.

"Well, that was this afternoon, and I felt good, even strong! I thought that this time it'd work out with Heather, and we'd be getting back together again, right? I made up my mind to go to Atlanta if she didn't want to come to Bigstone. Whatever."

She turned her gaze from the undulating water to me. She looked at me as if she were seeing me, really seeing me, for the first time. "We should have met a long, long time ago," she said sadly. "Before everything else happened."

She stared at the turbulent lake again. "I felt so good coming out of the session today, so refreshed. Like I'd been carrying a dead weight all this time, and now I was free of it. I know it sounds sappy, but that's just the way it was. I swear."

"So what happened?" I asked, knowing and yet not really wanting to know, not the details. "Why are you so miserable now?"

She took a deep breath an said, in a monotone: "While I was with my support group, feeling good, she met this baby dyke, and was feeling good, too, making a play for her, trying out her charms. I don't understand why she doesn't feel she gets enough love and affection and support from me, why she has to prove over and over again that she can be attractive and desirable to perfect strangers. I don't get it.

"And worst of all, I don't get why I stick around and take all this shit from her, why I don't just get the hell out and start living my own life again. I'm not just the woman Heather always keeps on the back burner for when there's no-one better around, right? I'm my own woman, too."

Then, turning to me again, she said, "Oh, Rosie. You're the one. You know that, don't you?"

Her eyes were soft and full of longing.

"You're depressed."

"I mean it. It's taken me all this time to come to terms with what I really felt for you all this past year, watching you fall for those Brill-creamed creeps and waiting for you to come to your senses, come to me."

I got up. "Dawn, you're raving. Why don't you go to the cabin and sleep it off?"

"I'm perfectly all right," she countered, getting up and hugging me. She didn't feel like a sister, the way her breasts were positioned between mine. "In fact, I've never been saner. I can see clearly now, as the song says. The rain has gone, the cobwebs have gone, the whole stupid game is over. Rosie, honey, sweetheart, I need you. Please!"

She kissed me powerfully, her mouth encircling mine. And then her tongue was prying my lips apart, and she was hungrily exploring my teeth, my inner cheeks, everything her tongue could reach as it frantically made its way inside.

My head reeled. She was a great kisser. I hugged her back, trying to keep up with her fire but finding that images of Calypso interfered.

She went on kissing me with passion, wrapping her legs around mine for closer contact.

"Oh, Rosie, Rosie," she whispered between kisses, caressing me all over with an urgency that left no doubt about what she was feeling. "We belong together, you and me. I should have come out to you a year ago. Then all this mess wouldn't have happened."

"What do you mean?" I asked, coming up for air.

"I mean that if I had told you I was lesbian when we first became friends, and if we'd become lovers then, everything would be different now. We'd be happy, together, rather than miserable, apart. Life is so unfair!"

I didn't know what to do, and I didn't know what to say.

I liked her very much, I felt very close to her, but I did not love her. Dawn was right. Life was unfair. Why did I still yearn for Calypso, whom I hated vehemently, rather than want to get involved with my best friend Dawn? Wouldn't it all be so much simpler, and wouldn't it be better all around, if I could go off into the Bigstone sunset with Dawn? Why couldn't I fall in love with my very best friend, my loyal, supportive, understanding, dependable Dawn?

We had always had a lot in common, or so I had thought. But now, sitting alongside her on the old wooden dock, in this strange place, I remembered all at once that Dawn had never had a boyfriend that I knew of, nor ever seemed interested in any man of mine. Could intimacy ever have been a possibility between us, then? I didn't think so.

"What do you say, sweetheart?" she persisted.

She clearly wanted an answer, and right away. I felt pressured. I was in no shape to make a life-choice.

"Dawn, Dawn, please, Dawn," I pleaded as gently as I could. "Let's not spoil a beautiful friendship by rushing into something that may not be right for us at all."

"Come on, Rosie," she said, grabbing me again and kissing me till my lips turned blue. "Sweetheart. Why are we torturing each other? Why can't we live happily ever after?"

I saw that it was not going to be easy to reason with her. She was sure that I was the answer to her every problem, while I knew that this just wasn't so. I felt sad, helpless, trapped. Should I make love with her to make her feel better, or should I tell her the truth and risk the end of our friendship?

She sensed my hesitation finally, and loosened her grip on my body. "I'm sorry. I don't know what got over me."

"Don't worry about it." I touched her cheek lightly, to show there were no hard feelings.

"Don't hate me, Rosie. It's just that I'm so . . . miserable!"

"It's all right."

For a while, we sat there together in the moon's glow, listening to the far-off sounds of the festival. At last, I felt that I should say something, make her know that we were still friends. I did like her, after all.

Then, all at once, I felt a wave of incredible tenderness wash all over me. Why the torture? I asked myself, looking into Dawn's red eyes, soft and sweet and full of compassion. Surely the best thing all around was for me to move in with Dawn and forget Calypso? That way I could have my cake and it eat, too. I could stay in Bigstone, apparently unchanged, near my family and friends. Wouldn't that be great? To all public intents and purposes I'd be the same old Rosie, but I'd be sharing Dawn's house. And why not? Wasn't it time to leave home and spread some independent wings? Who would ever suspect that we were lovers? The town was rife with gossip, but Bigstone gossip definitely lacked imagination. We would be safe.

Wordlessly, I got up and held out my hand for Dawn as she rose, too. As we walked back to the cabin, holding each other tenderly, each of us lost in thoughts and fantasies, these and other thoughts crowded my mind. The half-moon was directly overhead, smiling on us like a friend. All around us as we neared the cabin, women were walking in groups and in pairs towards the main stage.

This was the last night, the last nighttime concert, and it seemed that everyone was going. I wanted to join them.

But we were heading somewhere else, to our cabin. We were going to make love, expand and enhance our friendship. We were going to forget all the hurt and humiliation of the past few days. We were going to forge a future, establish a new connection, together.

Maybe this wasn't love, I told myself as we walked into the dark cabin. Maybe what it was, really, was a refuge, a haven for the walking wounded. So what? Surely those who came through, those who survived the scars, deserved some measure of calmness? Surely passion wasn't the only emotion that made the world go around?

Dawn swept me off my feet and carried me over the threshold into our half-cabin. From beyond the cloth partition, we could hear some heavy breathing. We were not alone.

Dawn set me down and closed the door behind us. I could see her smiling in the dark.

"This is a magical moment, Rosie," she said, kissing my neck tenderly. She held me in her powerful arms as if I were a fragile art object, more gently than I would have imagined. She was a big, strong woman, somewhat coarse in fact, but she undressed me surprisingly slowly and very, very gently, kissing every part of me as it became exposed. Then she quickly slid out of her overalls and pulled me towards Meg's mattress.

Her kisses were firmer than Calypso's, and her hands were stronger. She bit my lips and tugged at my nipples until they were more blue than red.

"Oh, Rosie, you are so sweet!" she mumbled as she bit my earlobe, then thrust her tongue inside and brought a shiver down my spine. "You have such supple breasts!"

She cupped her hands firmly around them and, with circular motions, gently ground them into my chest. For a minute, I felt the pain, but that sensation quickly gave way to another and I grabbed for her hair, pulling her urgently towards me and kissing her.

We hugged each other as we planted passionate kisses on each other's mouth. It seemed to me that I was drowning in her big, full lips. I felt as if I was out in stormy waters, drowning, yet the feeling was joyful and I was not scared at all. I knew that, in the end, I would come out of the waves strong and satisfied. This was an adventure, not a catastrophe.

Dawn was a very aggressive lover, and I had a hard time keeping up with her. I practiced everything Calypso had taught me, feeling both guilty and good about it, reasoning that she had it coming, for being so cruel. I made love with abundance, with a vengeance, with all the powers I could muster.

And then Dawn's fingers were parting my labia and flowing into me like wildfire. I felt a sweet, burning sensation as I gave out an involuntary moan. The women next door were also getting louder.

"Like that?" Dawn asked, pleased.

I moaned some more.

"Then you'll love this," she said, rubbing my clitoris.

"Oh, my God!"

Dawn laughed with glee. "Goddess, sweetheart," she said, and rubbed me more and more insistently. Then, as she slid two fingers inside, she announced triumphantly, "You're wet, and I'd love nothing better than to drown in you."

She rubbed me with increasing pressure, meanwhile sucking my breasts. I felt myself go limp as the fire swept all over my body. Dawn cupped my buttocks in her large hands and pressed me to her as I gave myself over to what I knew was the best orgasm of my life. I thought: who needs men, when women can give each other so much pleasure?

Dawn was glowing with gladness. "I can't believe how quickly you come. This is so terrific I could cry!"

And then she hugged me again, and burned her lips on mine once more before leading my own fingers on an expedition in search of her own orgasm. As I rubbed her with my fingers, her wetness increased and her breathing grew shorter and heavier.

I was amazed how happy I felt that my fingers could give such pleasure, and how Dawn's excitement rekindled mine. For a moment, both halves of the cabin reverberated with the urgent but contented moans of sexy women sharing their bodies with abandon.

Dawn screamed with joy, and I couldn't help feeling proud of myself. How wonderful it was to feel a woman's rippling orgasm, her wetness and her delight.

As we lay there, panting and grinning and hugging, I couldn't help thinking of Calypso, and feeling guilty. It was a bit ridiculous, I know, but while I was lying there on Meg's narrow mattress with Dawn around me like a blanket, I felt like a traitor to the one who had just betrayed me. Nothing made sense.

"This is the first time I ever made love with another

woman," Dawn confided with a wry smile, as if she was reading my mind. "It feels a bit strange, but terrific."

She kissed me again, and held me tighter.

But while Dawn's body felt comfortable against mine, and her lips felt sweet, nevertheless nothing she did could erase the love that I still felt for Calypso. Dawn may have been the answer to a cop-out prayer, someone to bring home to my parents without trouble, but she could not replace the woman I now knew more than ever was the only woman in my life.

Dawn sensed what was going on.

"There's nothing like the first time," she said with a sigh.

We smiled wistfully and hugged once more, sisters once more, then got up and got dressed in silence. The lovemaking next door was ebbing down to only a few nearly inaudible sighs of satisfaction.

We opened the door and went out again into the cool night air. A lazy wind moved a few treetops around.

"I wonder if anyone noticed we were gone," Dawn said, and her eyes twinkled in the moonlight. I could see that she could give Heather a run for her money if she asserted herself a bit more. Maybe they were better suited than either of them realized.

"Heather is probably combing the woods for you at this very minute," I joined the game.

"And finding all kinds of cute leprechauns to play with, no doubt, in the meantime. She's not very focused."

"You're not exactly one-tracked yourself," I pointed out.

She actually blushed. "With you, Rosie, it's not a passing fling. This was an exception."

"Maybe you should make an exception more often," I suggested slyly. "Give her a taste of her own medicine, so to speak."

"Think so?"

"Definitely."

We walked on towards the main stage. We could hear the music clearly now. It contrasted well with the rustle of the leaves.

"Who's singing?"

"I think it's Magic Megan and Moondust, sort of a New Age band," Dawn said. "They've just released their first album."

"Pretty good," I put in. I'd never heard anything like it. It was sort of classical, but had a mesmerizing beat, too.

We decided to get some ice cream before sitting down, so we stood in line again at the concession stand. Although it was chilly, many women were still bare-breasted. I found my mind, and eyes, wandering while we waited.

And then Heather was all over Dawn, kissing her and begging forgiveness. She physically separated us and I don't think it was entirely by accident that she kicked me while hanging from Dawn's stocky neck.

"Honey, it was only to make you jealous, to make you show me you care," Heather was saying. I couldn't believe anyone would ever fall for that line again, but Dawn seemed as happy as a pound puppy who'd just found a home.

"She looked cute," Dawn pouted, but softly, without anger.

"She was just a baby, Dawn. Give me a break."

"I can't go through these flings of yours any more," Dawn said, pushing Heather gently away while keeping her hand on her blouse. "It hurts."

"Oh, honey, I know. I know I make you miserable. I can't help it, they're so . . ."

Then, seeing the pained look in Dawn's eyes, she softened and drew nearer. "I promise, Dawn. I'll try. Okay? I'll really try. I swear there's nobody that holds a candle to you, honey. You're the one, the one and only. Give me a chance. Please?"

"I love you." Dawn's voice was almost a whisper now. She was probably crying. She wanted to believe Heather and I knew she'd do her best to be wooed back.

"Oh, honey, I love you so much! Please don't ever make me feel so lost and helpless again, I can't stand the thought of losing you."

As they kissed, so passionately that my heart did a cartwheel and my brain flashed Calypso before me like an after-image, I felt small, and unloved, and isolated all over again. I couldn't take it any more.

I decided to go over to the main stage area and hear, at long last, a concert of women's music.

After all, wasn't that the reason I'd come to the festival in the first place?

CHAPTER FOURTEEN

If Lavender Lizzie was right and there were, indeed, 4000 hot, red-blooded lesbians at the festival, then it seemed that just about all of them were present at the show that night.

I couldn't even begin to look for a place to sit in the crowd, so I decided to walk around and catch the music from the sidelines. After a bit of scouting, I found a spot from which to listen to the rest of the concert on my own.

I was impressed by the quality and variety of the music. I'd never even heard about any of these women singers and musicians before, and I wondered why. Why weren't they ever on the radio? Why was everything about this lesbian culture so wrapped up in secrecy? Why didn't these women get the recognition they deserved?

And then I remembered what Dawn had said about closets and I began to think how impossible it was for me ever to go back to Bigstone again. It wasn't my nature to hide. Of course, it had never been in my nature to have anything worth hiding, either. How could I tell my parents and siblings that I was a lesbian?

I did a double-take at my own audacity. And anyway, was I really a lesbian? I honestly couldn't say for sure, one way or the other, but for the first time that week I admitted to myself that, given the choice, I would be. But in Bigstone, I knew, there would be no choice: not because I would have to hide my true identity, but because I'd have nobody to bond with. Oh, I know, Dawn did say

that as many as seventy women in our town were lesbians, but I didn't believe her. And anyway, Miss Baxter
and her ilk never appealed to me and Miss Sawyer was
long gone.

Was I doomed? Was I going to end up like some Gothic
Miss Baxter, filing meaningless documents away in dusty
drawers and going home to a one-chair kitchen to drink
tea laced with brandy every night?

I was too young to be buried alive.

With an involuntary shudder, I concluded that I was
a creature of unleashed passions, that I wanted love and
fire in my life the way I had once craved cigarettes. I was
addicted.

I felt pretty depressed, but just when the blues threat-
ened to engulf me forever, I heard that familiar wild applause, hooting, and whistling that I immediately recognized from Lavender Lizzie's workshop. There, on the main
stage which I couldn't see, was someone the 4000 women
clearly liked very, very much.

I wondered who she was.

"How ya doin', ladies?" a nasal voice was asking.

The women whistled approvingly.

"As you know, each year at the end of the festival
we have two big surprises for you. The one that's coming
right up is the one I like the most, naturally, since I always get to introduce her and she's always sooooo cute.
Don't you agree, ladies?"

Again, the women hooted their favorable response.

"This year, she's sexy, vivacious, articulate, funny,
fun, and erudite. And very, very cute. Or did I mention
that already?"

As the crowd clapped enthusiastically, I wondered
if she was going to call Calypso to the stage. My heart
skipped at least two beats, but I remained where I was,
flushed in the face but well-hidden. I wasn't in the mood
for crowds.

Then the Mystery Woman's voice went on, and I understood the joke: she was the one she was introducing. The

119

crowd had seen the act before, but appreciated it again and again anyway.

"Welcome to the southernmost women's music festival in the world, honey," she said in one voice.

"Thank you, thank you. A pleasure to be here, I'm sure," she drawled with another.

"Okay, honey, the Amazons here are just dyin' t'know all about your impressions of this year's festival. Am I right, ladies? Tell me I'm right!"

The wild women clapped and whistled and hooted loudly. In fact, they stopped only intermittently as she spoke. Often, as her speech progressed, they laughed boisterously, and I even got some of the jokes myself.

"Thank you, thank you. Well. For five festive days, as you know, we have been celebrating KADZU. Kadzu is an age-old ceremony of women's music and crafts that we've been reviving for y'all right here in the heart of Dixie for the past five years. During Kadzu, hundreds of women-identified-women from all over the world descend on us. The tone of this year's festivities was set by Divine Dina, whose belly dance sent every navel within sight spinning throbbingly in harmonic vibration. The only unofficial participant, Lola Leather, mesmerized us with her version of Light My Pyre."

"That's a hot one, honey!" someone interjected.

"The Solisti di Salem, an English coven specializing in a capella realizations of figured bass runs immortalized by Suzi Quatro, was the crowd's favorite on the opening night."

"Don't ever close the night, honey! May it always stay open!" a couple of women called out in succession.

"Of course, as is the case every year, the classics were not neglected: an accordion quartet played a convincing, very vervy transcription of the Clara Schumann piano concerto. But for me, the highlight of the opening night was Deirdre, my Irish soul-sister. Like me, she came to the festival alone."

"You'll never walk alone, honey. Never again!"

"You're the greatest!"

"Anyway, it didn't take us long to discover that we had a lot in common, and to expand our common ground by carving out some private space along the lake.

"The second day was beautiful. There were workshops on everything you ever dreamed of, and in the afternoon, after a light lunch of bananas and coconut juice, there was a party on the lake. Baby dykes swayed to and fro to the tune of a bamboo band while we swam, sunbathed, or simply watched."

"And what an eyeful you are, honey!"

"The evening entertainment was spectacular: the stage was set to emulate the famous Harem of Susa in ancient Persia. Words can't begin to describe the power and sheer artistic stature of the event. Suffice to say that everyone paired off afterwards."

"Come soar with me, honey!"

"Deirdre and I rose early the next day — we had been volunteered to gather bananas for breakfast. While foraging in the woods, we came upon a magnificent sunrise over the lake. Ah, it was such a beautiful, poetic morning."

"Tell it like it is, honey!"

"And so the days went by: a multi-cultural exchange of lore and love. Imagine our surprise, then, when we found out that the festival was partly subsidized by the United Nations! Wait, wait, here's the story, as pieced together by Deirdre and me:

"When Myra Huntress and her lovers — I mean, partners! — first came up with the idea of this festival, they thought that it would be a good idea to apply for some grant monies. They wrote a few proposals, and heard nothing further from anyone . . . until they received a surprise grant from the United Nations for — get this — 'bridge-building between dykes.' "

The crowd really went wild on that one, and I smiled to myself, thinking: where does she get her ideas?

121

"It turned out that the United Nations gave Myra the money because it apparently believed that the project involved building concrete bridges between the chain of dykes that hold the raging rivers flowing into our mighty lake at bay. So anyway, the money was put in a trust fund, securing many future festivals.

"So put this on your calendar, all ye wilde witches and darling dykes: consecrate the last five days of the first month of spring to a celebration of women's music, dance, arts and crafts—whether you get to the festival or choose to celebrate it in bed. Indeed, however you choose to memorialize it, the KADZU festival is cause for great celebration year after year!"

The women gave the speaker an ovation that lasted several minutes. Then another woman took the stage, probably also one of the festival producers. This one spoke in a booming voice that did not unleash as many wild animals as her colleague had.

"Now comes the last item of business before we dance the final night away with The Loon in the Moon band: the woman who was so good on the day stage that we've invited her to sing one song for y'all on the night stage tonight! Ladies and broads, here she is, the newest southern singing sensation! And remember, years from now when her records out-sell mine—I'm joking, I'm joking!—remember that she was discovered right here at the southernmost women's festival. And now, let's give a rowdy welcome to—"

I couldn't make out the name, because the crowd went wild again as soon as she appeared on the stage. But when the din died down and she began to sing, there was no doubt in my mind that this was Calypso, that she had made it, that she was a star. Above the pain that still lingered, I felt happy for her.

The lyrics of her song drifted to me from the stage:

She blooms like a flower
She rises with the sun
She opens like a flower
Yes, she is the one

> She's the one and only in my life
> The one and only in this world of strife
> She's the one and only who can calm me down
> The one and only I want for my own

Flower child, child of the stars,
Let's pretend there are no ghosts around
Flower, flower, on the wall,
Who's the sweetest woman in the world?

> She's the one and only who can make me smile
> The one and only who can stay a while
> Yes, she's the one and only in my world of woe
> The one and only, Flower, please . . . don't go!

Darling Calypso! She had not only made it to the main stage, not only made her dream come true . . . she had also written a song for me, just like she promised she would. Could I really be so lucky? Was this song really for me, really about me? Did she really mean what she sang? Was there hope for us after all?

My heart was beating time with the music as I raced to the stage area. Like a woman possessed, I made my way through the crowd and came to a stop just below the flood-lights.

Someone tried to whisk me away, but I guess the wild look in my eyes gave her second thoughts, because she let me go. I stood below the stage like a devotee, my eyes fixed upon Calypso's lips as she sang.

She was too intent on her art to notice anything while she performed, but as soon as the song was over and the crowd burst into applause, she smiled and shifted her gaze.

Then she saw me, and took a step forward, and we seemed to freeze in space, two souls lost in limbo, together.

The crowd, noticing that something was happening, fell silent. Then, a couple of women moved forward and scooped me up on the stage. Like sleepwalkers, we moved

123

towards each other as if through fog, unbelieving and yet not wanting to test the vision by pinching ourselves awake.

And then she kissed me, and I kissed her, and the audience burst into wild applause, and I fainted.

CHAPTER FIFTEEN

I must have died and gone to heaven, because there I was, back in Calypso's bed, and she was there also, and just as happy to be with me as I was happy to be with her. Was I dreaming, or was I really back in Calypso's arms?

"Precious Flower," she whispered.

"I'm dreaming."

"Then so am I."

"I love you."

She kissed me. Her kiss spoke more clearly than words.

"I don't care what happens next, I don't care how crazy all this is, but I do love you. I don't know if this is the first time I've ever been in love, but I do know that this will definitely be the last."

She kissed me again.

"I'm dreaming," I mumbled. "This is too good to be true."

"What's too good to be true?" she asked.

"Us," I answered simply.

Calypso snuggled closer. "You mean this?" she asked, her lips encircling my nipples. "Or do you mean this?" she went on, and her tongue flicked over my breasts.

"Actually," I said, running my hands down her spine and towards her pear-perfect pair of buttocks, "I mean this."

She shivered slightly, and her legs parted languorously to welcome my hands.

"How about this?" she asked, folding her legs over my hands and massaging them with her thighs.

I smiled, and kissed her nose. "I love our bodies together. And your body . . . it's too good to be true."

"It's all done with mirrors," she agreed, licking the area between my breasts. "And silicone."

"Silicone Valley," I nodded, my head gently moving her face from my breasts to snuggle mine on hers. "Or should I rephrase that for accuracy, and say Silicone Mountains?"

She was smiling as I moved my lips up and down her topography, up and down and around her magnificent mammalian munificence. I wanted the journey to last forever, I wanted to memorize her every contour, every tiny hair and follicle, every pore and every mole. I wanted to make her happy.

"Mirror, mirror on the wall, who's got the biggest breasts of all?" she asked, and cupped her hands on mine for measurement.

"Big?" I asked, replacing my lips with my palms. "Who's talking big? We're talking beautiful. You have the most beautiful breasts in the universe, and that's a fact."

"I gather you've carried out a meticulous survey," she teased, squeezing my nipples.

"Ouch!"

"I'm a jealous woman," she continued, licking my wounds.

"So am I," I told her, kissing her eyes.

"You have the most amazing mouth in the world, you know that?" she asked, cupping my face and drinking my lips.

"Collagen," I intoned.

"Let's make sure never to run out," she suggested, and we kissed, and kissed again. Our lips blended together and our heartbeats kept up a persistent drumming.

"So," she said, coming up for air and lying on top of me. "Is this love?"

"Whatever it is," I smiled, "it's great sex."

"Is sex love?"

And it hit me, her fragility and sense of panic, her need not to get involved, not to get hurt. She wanted to know what would happen once the festival closed the next afternoon, if I'd be there for her or be gone.

But before I could tell her how much I loved her, and that I'd never leave, she was cool, calm, and collected again.

"Damn right," she said, kissing my underarms and pinning down my breasts with hers. "Great sex. Let's enjoy it."

And we did.

After we'd rehearsed everything that we'd shared the night before, and a few new tactile messages of lust, Calypso turned around again to nibble my toes.

I moaned with pleasure.

"Wait," she whispered. "There's more to come."

She did not stop at my toes, but kissed my shins, and my thighs, slithering over my enraptured body like some fantastic animal. I felt wet all over.

"There's a lot more to come, sweet Flower," her silken voice went on as she sank her mouth into the warm wetness that had been shielded by my pubic hairs.

As my breathing grew heavier and my head grew lighter, she began to lick me, gently and insistently, her tongue finding places inside me that had never been explored before.

Dawn's fingers had been wonderful, it's true, but Calypso's lips were heaven-sent. She fondled my breasts as she licked me, and I began to moan to her rhythm.

I felt as if my body, wet as an ocean, was suddenly overcome by an earthquake that began at the very bottom and then overtook the sky. I was shaking and crying and happy and ecstatic all at once. Finally, I convulsed, screaming, then came down to rest in Calypso's amazing arms.

"Sweetheart," I whispered over and over again. "That was so wonderful. I love you so much!"

She brushed my hair from my face and kissed me gently.

We lay there together, limb on limb and hearts entwined, until my breathing returned almost to normal. Then, Calypso rolled me over and repositioned her own mesmerizing body over my tongue with small, steady, dance-like movements.

Feverishly, I licked her, finding her juices strangely sweet and sour and scented. I loved loving her.

The next thing I knew, she, too, was shaking and trembling all over, as wave upon wave of her pleasure was washing over me. I felt as she felt, the tidal wave of her ecstasy cascading all over my trembling body. I heard her moaning, over and over again, and it was the most beautiful song she'd ever written, melodious and sure.

We hugged again, drowning in our emotions. Then, just when I thought we'd relax ourselves to sleep, we made love again, with great passion. It was as if the stars found their right niche in the sky and the earth revolved on its proper axis, everything was so right, so perfect.

Afterwards, as we lay together on the bed, breathing in harmony and staring at the half-moon beyond the pink blinds, Calypso turned to me and asked, "Wanna dance?"

"Here?"

"No. There. Let's go to the dance. It'll be going on all night. I want to celebrate where it all began."

"I didn't know you were a romantic," I said, running a finger gently down her sensuous spine.

"And I took you for a casual explorer, a voyeur," Calypso replied, wrapping her wondrous arms around me again. "I guess we were both wrong."

"And yet so right," I mused, kissing her hair. "We are so right for each other."

"Right now, I feel like dancing," she said, getting up and throwing my clothes over my head playfully. "Let's go."

We got dressed and got out, hugging each other ecstatically all the way. The short walk to the stage area seemed like a transcontinental trek.

The music was electrifying, but I can't tell you anything about the band because I hardly noticed anything except Calypso. Her perfume smelled like sandalwood incense. It wafted into my brain like a drug, making me totally oblivious to anything else. The music was very danceable and we danced for a long time.

It was wonderful to feel the presence of so many hundreds of women dancing together all around us, creating a huge, special place where it was not only safe, but stupendous, to be lesbian. I felt like an initiate in a cult so mysterious, so secret, that discovering it is a very special privilege, and becoming one with it is intoxicating.

Even when the music was loud and fast and we hardly touched, the gossamer threads of our passion held us together like the most powerful glue. When the music was soft and slow, our bodies fused in the fire, passionately entwined in a bond that only lightning could tear asunder. And I wasn't too sure about lightning, either.

When, hours later, the band stopped playing and the last of the dancers moved towards the exits, there was Dawn beside us. She placed a hand on my shoulder and whispered, "Thanks. You're the best."

I turned to see her and Heather, holding hands and smiling as happily as ever. It didn't even cross my mind to wonder what had become of Malibu.

"I've decided not to go back to Bigstone tomorrow," Dawn announced. "The way I feel right now, I may never go back there again. Except to visit you," she added quickly. "I'll write you and let you know what's up, all right?"

"I'm happy for you, Dawn," I said, and meant it.

We must have hugged a bit too fondly, for both Heather and Calypso cut in.

"Tell the factory I've quit, I've died, I've gone religious, anything," Dawn went on, hugging Heather tightly, then planting a kiss on her lover's lips for good measure. "I've told Meg and Cathy that I'm not going back with them, but don't worry, they're all set to drive you back after lunch."

"Thanks."

I tried not to look at Calypso. There was a whole lot of stuff still unresolved and unspoken, but we had the rest of the night to decide things. "I'll look for them," I promised.

"And y'all should come on down and visit us in Atlanta real soon, y'hear?" Heather put in. "We've got lots of room, so don't be shy."

We parted as good friends, knowing that our paths were no longer so sure of intersecting, but wanting nevertheless to preserve something of our special feelings for each other, some sense of sharing, caring, respect. Many things were left up in the air between us, there was no time to talk, but nevertheless we knew, wherever we were, that our friendship was on firm ground. We would always be there for each other.

CHAPTER SIXTEEN

Calypso and I walked slowly back, savoring the coolness of the air, the darkness of the night, and the heat generated by our interlocking fingers.

I steered her to the lake, to which I felt a real attachment by now, a strong bond.

"This is my favorite place, like a home away from home."

"The water's great," she agreed. "I love swimming here."

"Yeah," I said, my thoughts wandering.

"I most especially liked swimming that day," she went on, reading my faraway thoughts, "when you played so hard to get, so damn independent, smoking as if you didn't care."

"I cared, all right. But I was scared."

"And what do you take me for, Fearless Fodsicka?"

I hugged her more tightly. "No, not fearless. Flawless."

She pushed me gently away from her. "I'm no more flawless than you are."

"I couldn't get you out of my mind the minute you asked me to dance that night," I told her as we walked, hugging each other's so-familiar body, tightly, along the old dock.

"You're kidding."

"It's true. I was totally smitten, but I had no way of understanding what it meant, what it was all about."

"Something good, anyway," she said.

"Yes, something wonderful."

And then she sang me a bit from that song "Some Kind of Wonderful," a song which now took on a new meaning, as if it had always been written for one woman to sing to another.

We kissed again, and I marvelled again how her lips sent shivers down my spine each and every time.

I told her.

"I'm not exactly immune either, you know," she laughed. She kissed my neck and, just before pulling away again, bit it lightly. "Don't mind me. It's just an old vampire trick I once picked up. From a rabid bat."

"Did it land on your head, or what?"

"Quite a concussion, you're right."

"Ouch."

"I love punning with you, laughing with you, loving you . . . " She grew silent again.

"I love you," I said. "I love you so much!"

"Who said anything about love?" she shot back.

We looked at each other then, carefully and hard, aware of how tender was the shoot of feelings we had planted in each other. The unanswered questions still left unasked between us were crowding us again, demanding space. For a minute, we were about to speak, to play at reality for a while, but then we breathed in and breathed out and the moment was gone.

There would be time for them later. Now, there was only time for making love.

I woke up happy. The sun filtered through the blinds, gently coercing my eyelids to open. I jumped out of bed and went to the window to look out at yet another perfect summer day. "What are you doing up so early?" Calypso asked, standing by my side and kissing the nape of my neck.

I hugged her. "Isn't it beautiful?"

"Mmmm. And so are you. Come back to bed, Flower. We have some unfinished business to take care of. Know what I mean?"

"What do you mean?" I teased, tickling her elbow.

She took my hand and led me back to the ruffled sheets. She threw herself on the bed and scooped me in on top of her.

"I mean this," she said, kissing me gently on the lips, and then again, more firmly. "And I mean this," she added, caressing my breasts. "And I don't mean to stop."

"That's fine with me," I said, rolling Calypso over and hugging her. I kissed her body from forehead to lips, from ear to lips to ear, from breast to breast, as she caressed me and kissed me with more and more purpose and with more and more strength.

It was almost dawn when we finally surrendered passion to sleep. Then, with the morning sun, our passions rekindled.

I felt my chest contract, then melt. My heart felt airy, as if it was soaring to meet the sun's finger-like rays. Then I felt Calypso's touch on my skin, and it was the sun's touch: warm, soothing, alive, trembling with a sort of subdued excitement that could become unleashed at any moment.

"I love you," I whispered over and over again, "I love you, I love you, I love you."

"Oh, my sweet wild virgin," she whispered back, kissing my palms. "We have set free a wild and wonderful animal here."

"A flower, sweetheart," I told her between kisses. "Petal by petal, Calypso, you have unfurled a flower."

"Flower," she echoed. "Would you mind if I pick you up?"

"You'd better!" I said, hugging her with all my strength. "Don't you know that every petal thanks you for its liberation?" I added, kissing her fingers one by one.

"Tell me more."

"Your body smells of morning, of sweet promise."

She was silent again. Had I said something wrong?

Her fingers played with my hair. "How did the poet put it? Promises to keep, miles to go before sleep, etcetera."

"Take whatever path you choose, so long as all your roads lead to me." I felt my heart leap, and a great joy sweep over my body. "Let me be there for you, wherever you go, whenever you come to rest. Let me grow at your feet and tickle your sleep."

"You're sweet."

"Smell me."

She smiled again, and her eyes seemed to clear. "You're a very special flower," she said, positioning herself on my back and proceeding to massage my shoulders. "A wild mountain flower that is not quite a rose and not quite a rhododendron, neither phlox nor ladyslipper, not exactly a lily and not a jane-in-the-pulpit, either"

With every flower she named, she gave me a kiss, and her magical hands massaged my back lower and lower, sending stimulating messages to my increasingly excited brain.

"You are not quite like a daffodil, neither are you like the heather. You're not a pansy, a daisy, or an aster, nor are you a honeysuckle — though that's pretty close, come to think of it," she added, her lips upon my buttocks and her hands cupping my breasts from behind.

I moaned with pleasure.

"Flower," she went on. "An unnamed, soon-to-be-tamed flower. A rare flower that, like the phoenix, rises from the ashes only once in a thousand years," she said, rolling me over and then sucking my breasts.

I thought my heart would surely stop beating right then and there, but even as it pounded noisily in my ears, I found the strength and the presence of mind to crush her intoxicating body into mine and to kiss her breasts and hair and face and arms all over, over and over again.

Hugging, kissing, and licking, each of us felt her heartbeat quicken, her soul fly, until — oh, so together! — we felt the sweet juicy release of tension and, almost at once, an overwhelming surge of caring and gladness, too.

Exhausted and completely satisfied, we rolled away from each other. But immediately, our skins felt totally naked and exposed, so we groped for each other again, snuggling tightly and facing each other for yet another, yet strangely new, string of kisses. There was no end in sight for our passion, for our need to touch and love each other.

A long time later, relaxed and comfortably enfolded within the crook of Calypso's arm, I couldn't help but say out loud the words which had been welling within me all night.

It was time to broach the taboo subject. I began indirectly: "This is wonderful, and this is sad, and I'm wildly happy, happy, happy."

She nodded. "Me, too."

I looked at her, and felt so much love for her that I nearly cried. "So what do we do?"

"This does mess things up a bit, doesn't it?" she intoned softly. "And yet, it is a shared moment of magic, isn't it?"

I held her snugly and sighed. Was she thinking what I was thinking? Dare I hope?

"Let's not think about our parting, okay?" she went on. "Let's just think about the few hours we still have together."

I couldn't speak, my heart was so noisy, but I managed to kiss her deeply again.

"I only said 'I love you' once before in my life," she told me then. "To my first lover."

She grew silent.

"Did she hurt you very much?"

She nodded.

"I'm not her, Calypso. I'm me. I love you. I can't think of doing anything without you, of going anywhere without you, of loving anyone but you, ever."

She sighed, and took my hand in hers.

We sat together on the bed, watching the sun rise through the trees, in silence. I was afraid she'd break the spell, that she'd break down and break away. But deep down, I didn't think it was really possible that our bodies could communicate so well and then words would come in between and tear us apart.

I waited for Calypso to speak, and finally she did.

"I love you, you know that, don't you?"

I hugged her more closely, tears welling in my eyes. We hugged, then kissed tenderly again. Before we were fully aware of what was going on, we were making love again, hungrily devouring each other's body and licking each other's warm, juicy regions. We orgasmed one after the other, then hugged tightly.

I thought we'd never leave the bed, but then Calypso said, "Let's get some breakfast. I'm famished."

I pulled her closer, not wanting to part for anything, and murmured, "Hey, we have to talk."

"Flower, I'm starving. Let's eat."

"Okay," I said, getting up. She was very moody, I could sense that. "Let's eat."

She led the way to the kitchen and rummaged around noisily for something to whip up.

"This is serious, honey," I pleaded as I watched her opening and closing jar after jar, box after box. "Please. Let's talk. I have to know if you want me to stay, or go away again, or what."

She looked down at the jar she was holding and suddenly sat down and cried. I sat down beside her and kissed her eyes dry.

Sniffing, she kissed the palms of my hand again, very gently. "The timing's lousy, you know that? How can I ask you to change your plans, to change your life, leave your entire past behind and stay?"

I clasped her hand, pulled her to me and hugged her. In a minute, we were all over each other, all over the floor, kissing again and again and again.

"Sweet Calypso," I said. "Can't you see? I can't leave now! The past is just that, and the future is you. I love you and I'm going to stay as long as we both feel this way about each other."

She hugged me close, and said to my hair, "I'm scared. We hardly know each other, we haven't really talked. What if it all wears away in a week and gets washed back to the sea with the next storm? I've had too many disappointments to risk getting involved again."

"I love you," I said, kissing her mouth. "Nothing on this planet is etched in stone, I know that, but what I feel and what you feel and what we feel together is real. My life till now was just a sleepwalking session, I didn't do anything but breathe in and out and watch the sun rise and set. You know what I mean?"

She nodded, caressing my arms.

"And this weekend, my whole world changed. I'm not talking only about us, about finding the passionate place in my soul. That's wonderful and special and it makes me very, very happy, but it's more than that, it's like finding that I was raised by a bunch of butterflies, and really I'm a . . . a robin, a whole different sort of flying object! You know what I mean! I'm me, and I'm glad I found out what my real identity is."

Calypso kissed me. "A flying flower. Mmmm."

"I'm serious! And while it would have been terrific enough just to find my true identity, something even more wonderful happened to me, and that's you, and this festival, and finding a whole huge family to share the rest of my life with."

"I'm jealous already," she said, playfully nibbling my ear.

"Nothing to be jealous of," I replied seriously, hugging her closer and closer till I thought we'd merge. "I love you. I want to spend the rest of my life with you. I love your music, and I want to find what my own real talent is, too, and pursue it."

"You should be a writer," she said, kissing me deeply. "You have an interesting way with words."

"Writer, baker, cabinetmaker, who cares?" I said, running my hands around her breasts. "We've got a long and terrific lifetime ahead of us, sweet Calypso. Together!"

"Sounds good," she said, and her eyes softened.

"Believe it!" I said with conviction.

"And now let's eat," she said. "I'm really starving."

So I leaned against her, and we made love again. There were two hours to the end of the festival, and two hours could last a very long time.